ALIAS

TRACY ALEXANDER

Piccadilly
PRESS

First published in Great Britain in 2015
by Piccadilly Press
Northburgh House, 10 Northburgh Street,
London EC1V 0AT

A CIP catalogue record for this book
is available from the British Library.

ISBN: 978–1–848–12444–8

1 3 5 7 9 10 8 6 4 2

Typeset by Palimpsest Book Production Limited,
Falkirk, Stirlingshire

Printed and bound by Clays Ltd, St Ives Plc

www.piccadillypress.com

Piccadilly Press is part of the Bonnier Publishing Group
www.bonnierpublishing.com

Thanks to Nadia the astute, Behzad the wary,
Chloe for the gen on Leeds and pithy Jackie.

Newswire — 4 Sept 21:46 UTC

IBB, YEMEN — The CIA has declined to comment on reports of a drone strike in the Ibb province of Yemen. Several missiles were fired, killing two members of the same family who were working in the fields of a remote village. A local source said, 'Yesterday's victims were a grandmother and her granddaughter — they were picking okra. We are simple farmers. The only thing people here know about America is that it kills our people. American drone strikes do not fight terrorism, they fuel it.'

Despite President Obama's announcement that no strikes would be authorised unless there is 'near certainty that no civilians would be killed or injured', this is the eleventh confirmed drone strike in Yemen this year. Civilian deaths as a result are estimated at between 17 and 33, including 3 children.

PART 1

1

I got to school to find Lucy rummaging through her locker like it was a lucky dip.

'What have you lost this time, Lucy?'

'That chemistry sheet. Chambers'll kill me.'

'You'll be all right,' I said. 'He's in a good mood today.'

'How d'you know?'

'I read his horoscope.'

'Did you read mine?'

'Yep. You're going to lose your chemistry homework.'

The usual banter.

I dumped my books, got what I needed for the morning's lessons and went into our classroom, followed by Lucy. Chambers came in a few minutes later.

'Good morning, 11.2.'

A few people grunted.

'Any forms for the Spanish trip on my desk, please. My chemistry class – your sheet on electrolysis is due in *today*.' He pushed his floppy fringe out of the way. 'Right. Registration.'

He raced through our names, just managing to get

to the end – Wilks – as the bell went for first period. There was the usual crush as thirty people tried to squeeze out of the door at once – some people can't learn. *I* waited for Lucy.

'Mr Chambers, I'm sorry, I left my homework at home,' she said.

'Did the dog eat it?'

'He hadn't when I left,' said Lucy.

Chambers grinned.

'Tomorrow, without fail. Understood?'

'Yes, Mr Chambers.'

'Told you,' I said as we fought our way along the corridor.

Lucy jokes that I'm telepathic. I'm not, obviously. I pay attention, that's all.

Chambers always has a kink near the bottom of his right trouser leg when he cycles to school because he wears a clip. That only happens on Mondays, Tuesdays and Fridays – he must need a car on the other days, or maybe his wife needs his bike. He never cycles if it's wet or windy. If he arrives by bike he is noticeably more cheerful, at least to start with. It was a still, sunny Monday at the end of September. Not magic, logic.

It's a habit now, being aware of everyone and every-thing, but wasn't always.

When I was small, Mum used to say I lived in a world of my own, because I'd spend hours making up stories with my dolls and Build-A-Bears. Before I went to school she had an attack of conscience and a trail of kids came round to play with me, but I either ignored them or told them off for touching my toys. If that made Mum worry that I'd find it hard to mix, she needn't have. At school it was too noisy to think, so I joined in like everyone else – but I didn't care who I played with. It was the games that were fun.

That changed when Lucy and I got thrown together. We were the most frequent visitors to the library, because we'd both read all the books in the classroom. On our journeys across the playground she'd update me on the story she was writing about a robot girl. I was Impressed, capital I. When she asked me round after school, I asked Mum to plait my enormously long hair – the eight-year-old's version of making an effort.

At home, I ate my tea in front of the telly – except on Sundays when Mum cooked a roast. But at Lucy's it was all laid out with serving dishes and a water jug, and her mum sat at the table with us. I was carefully winding my spaghetti round my fork, listening to Lucy's two older brothers joshing, when she asked, 'So . . . where does your father come from, Samiya?'

'Yemen,' I said.

'I'm never quite certain where that is,' she said.

'Under Saudi Arabia,' I replied, remembering Dad pointing it out before one of the trips he made there every few years.

'Gosh!'

'But my mum's from Wales,' I said, as though it might help.

'How on earth did they meet?' she asked, as though it was the marriage of an alien and a mushroom.

I wanted to say, 'Not telling you, you nosy cow,' but I didn't. I told her that they met at Amir and Diana's wedding.

Even though my face was the only coffee in a class full of vanilla milkshake, no one had ever made a big deal about it. But Lucy's mum was on a roll. Her interrogation covered dress, food, alcohol and praying. I felt more foreign with every answer, despite the fact that we watched *Pointless*, ate egg and chips and only prayed when the lottery numbers were drawn. Lucy was swapping looks with her brothers that I couldn't decipher, which made me even more uncomfortable. I remember bolting the chocolate pudding, desperate to get back to the solar system we'd made and show Lucy that inside I was just like her – but Mum arrived and whisked me off home.

Lying in bed, my logical brain decided that if being different was a problem, I wouldn't be different.

Making sure I blended in wasn't rocket science –
like what they like
laugh at the same things
don't have falafel in your lunchbox
get a haircut.
And the results were pretty remarkable –

Lucy and I became inseparable *and* party invitations began to arrive in my book bag on a regular basis. For the first time ever I was in the thick of things. So I carried on.

By the time I moved up to secondary school I'd learnt more than any SAT paper could measure. I scrutinised everything from conversations and body language to tics and accents. I noticed the way people used their hands and how often they mirrored each other. Posture, swallowing, sweatiness – you name it, I logged it. It was a game of sorts. I knew when my history teacher had been in the gym from the way she walked, and was the only one not surprised when the IT guy started going out with Miss Hicks. The constant vigilance was exhausting, but worth the rewards.

I'd discovered a way of dealing with the world, which, in the end, turned out to be a way of changing it.

2

After October half-term, Chambers' class got two new additions – twins, called Hugo and Juliette. They were white-blond and perfectly polished, like albino Persian cats.

I studied them that first morning, delighted they were in my maths set. *They* looked less than delighted, hardly acknowledging the rest of the class. That should have made me dislike them, but it did the opposite. They fascinated me.

I jostled my way through the crowd to get next to them in the lunch queue, armed with the opening line of my campaign to make them love me. There was no point trying to be the same – the twins were unique. So . . .

'Are you in witness protection?' I asked, with a serious face. There had to be a flipping good reason for pitching up halfway through GCSEs.

There was silence . . . and then Hugo laughed.

'I wish we were. What do you think we witnessed?' He paused. 'Or do you think *we're* the criminals, snitching on our unsavoury chums?'

'Criminals, definitely,' I said. 'I'm guessing protection racket.'

'Because we look so menacing?' he said, looking anything but.

'Exactly.'

'Why are lies always so much better than the truth?'

'Because they're not true,' I said.

'Tell me a lie about you.' He stared at me with his watery-blue eyes. It was intoxicating.

'This is my third life,' I said. 'I remember all my previous reincarnations.'

It was the start of a surreal conversation that only ended because the dinner ladies ushered us out.

'We like you,' said Hugo. 'Don't we, Juliette?'

Juliette tucked a strand of her razor-sharp bobbed hair behind her ear.

'We do.'

That was it – I attached myself to them, like a barnacle.

They'd been at school about a month when the Head randomly banned charity wristbands, saying they were 'a breach of the uniform policy'. Hugo was outraged, even though he didn't own one. In our library period he pulled out his iPad Air and announced, 'Samiya, we're going on strike.'

'Like the miners?'

'Is that the extent of your knowledge?'

I got a discourse on the right to strike while he set up a Facebook event called 'United We Bargain'.

'What does that mean?'

'That together we're strong, and the Head has to negotiate with us. It's borrowed from the trade union movement.'

'It's weird that you know all that stuff.'

'It's *history*, you dim girl. It's what made us.'

That week, Hugo spent every break time lobbying – Year 7s, prefects, the kids who smoked over by the far hedge. I trailed around after him, translating his spin into plain English. On Friday, instead of going to assembly, a third of the school gathered outside in the freezing cold to listen to him.

'. . . wearing the wristbands not only benefits the individual charity but prompts discussion, which helps develop well-balanced and thoughtful pupils.'

It was like being addressed by a Nordic superhero, complete with perfect Tintin quiff. The Head had no choice but to cave.

The kids lower down the school idolised Hugo, but to our year he was Marmite. I could see why – he didn't care what he said or who he upset and was far too full of himself. But he was also gorgeous. And I was drawn to him like a magnet. The closer we got, the less time I wasted analysing what he said and did. He wasn't interested in flattery, didn't care if we disagreed. He didn't even mind if we were silent. We were yin and yang.

The downside to our friendship was that the twins lived miles away, near Twyford, so I only saw them at school. Lucy said they were vampires, tucked away in farming country so they could feed on the cattle. I told Hugo and he said she was right, but they preferred pigs — ideally pot-bellied.

When our GCSEs finished in June, the summer seemed full of opportunity. The twins could come over. I could go there . . . Hell, I'd have oiled the chain and adjusted the gears on my ancient bike if it meant I could see where they lived! But that didn't happen.

Five days into the holidays, Dad plonked a printed-out itinerary on the breakfast table.

'The holiday of a lifetime,' he said, beaming.

Mum took his hand.

'We're going to Yemen, to see your dad's side of the family.'

There'd been almost comic signs that they were up to something — abruptly ending hushed conversations and tilting the family laptop so the screen was obscured — but I didn't expect to be teleported to the desert.

'It's a special chance, Samiya,' said Dad. 'A whole month together.'

The idea made me instantly claustrophobic.

'It's not exactly Florida!' I said.

Dad took the crumpled photo of his mum out of his wallet. She looked like she'd been was cut out of a *National Geographic* — dressed in black, with really wrinkled skin, and more gaps in her smile than teeth.

'At last, you'll meet your grandmother.'

I carried on eating my Weetabix.

As soon as Dad left for work, Mum had a go at me.

'You did a good job of putting a damper on things, Samiya.'

'Do we really have to go for so long?' Moody voice. 'Only I've made plans with Lucy . . . and the twins.'

'The twins you're so friendly with that *I've* never met them?'

Mum's logic was flawed. In sixteen years, *I'd* never met my Yemeni relatives, but *they* were suddenly so important I had to spend my whole summer with them.

'I just think you and Dad could have asked me first.' *Fat chance!*

The visas had come the day before. The flights were booked for Saturday. It was a coup. That three's a crowd was certainly true in our house.

As we boarded the plane, I said my goodbyes on Facebook, Instagram and Snapchat . . . and nothing was ever the same again.

3

Before we landed at Sana'a, Mum gave me a navy headscarf to wear. Hers was grey, which suited her bright-blue eyes. I went to the loo to see what I looked like – it was strange the way it changed me. Slightly scary, or maybe it was the whole situation that was slightly scary.

According to Hugo, Yemen was cripplingly poor, life expectancy was sixty-two and everyone was either a militant or a farmer. I was dreading it. If Mum and Dad hadn't been so jolly I might have tried to tell them how I was feeling, but they were acting like we were on our way to Disneyland!

Stepping out of the aeroplane was like walking into the nozzle of a giant hairdryer, set to maximum everything. A cousin of Dad's met us. Despite his traditional dress, the way his red-and-white headdress was flicked over his ears made him look jaunty. He whisked us off to his car, putting his shades on as soon as we were outside. It was surreal hearing him and Dad jabbering away. Mum and I sat in the back and I must have dropped off, because the next thing I knew the car had stopped and there was a face pressed against my window. It took all my willpower not to cry out.

'It's all right,' said Mum, patting my arm. 'It's a check-point.'

We had to show our passports and permits. I stared at the back of the driver's seat because I didn't want to look at the guns the police – or whoever they were – were carrying.

That happened a few times. I kept expecting to be dragged from the car and denounced for pretending to be a Muslim.

At some point we started to climb, driving up dirt tracks at speed. It felt as if one accidental twitch would send us careering down the hillside to certain death. I was silent, wishing I was safe at home, slobbed out on the sofa, counting the days until my GCSE results like everyone else. Yemen was more than foreign – it was alien.

The journey eventually ended in a village made up of buildings clinging to the side of the steep slope, with a fancy minaret in the middle. It would have been grand, if it hadn't looked as though the whole lot might crumble at any minute. We were welcomed by what must have been the whole population. It was like we were celebrities – people pushed through the crowd to touch us, shake our hands, stroke my face . . . I had to make myself not flinch.

I met my dad's brothers and sisters and a hundred cousins and their children, and some grandchildren. Mum slipped out of view, swallowed up by the sea of people. It was all a bit much, what with the oven-like heat and the chatter I couldn't understand and the smell – ripe and raw and foul and sweet all at the same time.

A girl about my age, wearing a white hijab, spoke to Dad before taking my hand and leading me away through a web of alleys. I didn't want to go, but there didn't seem to be an easy way to refuse. She repeated the same words again and again, but it meant nothing to me. Every time we turned I tried to find a landmark that would help me find my way back to Mum and Dad – the empty baskets all in a pile, the washing line hung from two windows, the man asleep, cross-legged, with a shiny dagger tucked into his waistband.

The girl stopped in a doorway and, when I hesitated, pushed me inside.

'Samiya,' the girl said loudly.

A wrinkly hand stretched out to take mine. I didn't want to but was just about well brought up enough to take the hand. The old lady stood up agonisingly slowly, as though she needed oiling. She let go of my hand and reached up to cup my face in her palm, saying something to me that I wished made sense. She was tiny, only reaching my shoulder. I stared at her, because I couldn't look anywhere else. She was the photo from Dad's wallet. I smiled. And so did she. Being almost toothless didn't make her smile any less affecting. Tears began to pour down her face. I felt myself join in.

'*Jaddah*,' she said. '*Jaddah*.'

I nodded.

'Grandmother,' I said. And then, '*Jaddah.*'

The girl that brought me, who was grinning away, took my grandma's hand and repeated, '*Jaddah.*' I got it. We shared a grandma. She was my cousin.

'Lamyah,' she said.

I repeated her name, 'Lamyah.'

We traded English and Arabic words – house, village, chicken, Dad – mimicking each other, and ended up laughing. The joy was completely contagious.

That was all it took for the wizened nut-brown stranger, shrouded in black, and the girl in the white hijab to become part of my family. There must be something chemical, to do with having the same genes, because from then on nothing felt quite so alarming.

That first night we ate some kind of stew outside with about twenty strangers that Dad called our 'close' family. I sat between *Jaddah* and Lamyah. There wasn't a moment when one of them wasn't telling me something. It didn't matter that I couldn't understand what. Like them, I ate with my right hand. (Dad had briefed me on the plane – left hand for wiping your bum, right hand for everything else.)

I was so desperate for sleep when the party eventually broke up that I didn't mind the mattress on the floor, even when I discovered I was sharing with Lamyah and Maryam *and* that the animals were tucked up on the floor below.

* * *

The next day I chose to hang around with *Jaddah*, helping her cook. Mum and Dad made bad jokes about me poisoning the village, but left me to it. At home I was never interested, but there's a world of difference between opening a packet from Tesco and making food from things you've picked (or slaughtered) yourself. I chopped green stuff while *Jaddah* pulled apart a goat. I was rather proud that I managed not to gag. After that, we swept the floors and I beat the bedding with Lamyah. Hugo would have called me a skivvy. The idea of him wouldn't sit properly in my head, so I tucked him away.

In the afternoon, while I used sign language and a few basic words to talk to Lamyah and some of the other girls, the men sat chewing khat – Dad included. He said it was traditional. I said it was drugs. They looked funny, chewing away, the balls of leaves making one cheek bulge like a hamster.

It was nice seeing Dad back where he belonged. A part of me that I had always found irrelevant became something to celebrate.

Days went by. The whole community just got on with the routine of living. Herding goats. Picking vegetables. I even milked a cow, pretty unsuccessfully. More successful were my cooking lessons. *Jaddah* taught me to make all sorts, but my favourite was the bread with a hot egg and coriander middle.

I quickly got to know the other teenagers, who all seemed a lot more grown up than me. We took long walks, stopping in the shade where I gave English lessons. Hilarious. You wouldn't think you could joke with people who don't share your language, but you can. I taught them text talk.

LOL. OMG. YOLO.

Although I slept at Dad's sister's, we visited every other house in the village, drinking tea and doling out the gifts we'd brought with us – T-shirts, belts, jewellery, make-up and, bizarrely, watches. Time didn't seem to matter – except for when the call to prayer rang out and everything stopped.

It was a beautiful place, like Dad said it would be – very green and totally wild. (Nothing like a desert.) I felt completely at home, which made no sense to me at all. And didn't want to leave, which made no sense to Mum (who, after three weeks on a floor, missed her bed) or Dad (who was itching to get back to pre-season football training). It was hard to put into words . . . I suppose I felt special.

After days of begging, driving Mum and Dad crazy, they finally agreed I could stay on. I waved them off without a care.

From the minute they left, Lamyah and I were hardly ever more than a metre apart – which was odd, given how much I liked my own company. We were busy all day, tended to spend the evening with *Jaddah* – I taught her to play charades using Lamyah as a very bad translator – and slept like the dead. In the nanosecond between awake and coma, I imagined living in the village for real.

Way too soon, the day came for me to be driven back to the airport. I made Lamyah promise to come and visit me ASAP. (*Jaddah* said she'd never left the mountain and wasn't going to – at least, I think that's what she said.) The whole village came to see me off, but I only had eyes for Lamyah and *Jaddah*. Their weeping faces were engraved on my retina.

4

Arriving back in Buckingham at the beginning of August, everything was Strange, capital S. Or maybe I was. Mum and Dad had slotted straight back into the routine, clearly pleased to be home. I felt the opposite – as though I'd left something behind, which I had. Getting a date in the diary for Lamyah to come to England was all I could think about.

'What about Christmas?' I said to Dad at breakfast – thirty-six hours after touching down at Gatwick airport. 'It might even snow!'

'It's not that simple, Samiya. She'd need a passport and a visa . . . someone to travel with . . .'

'We can arrange that, can't we?'

Dad's body language was less than enthusiastic. He disappeared off to work, muttering something about 'next year'. He could mutter all he liked. If necessary, I'd sort it out myself.

I got dressed and went to meet the twins, feeling slightly uneasy. Six weeks and three days without a text or a Snapchat was forever . . .

For once, only Hugo turned up.

'No Juliette?'

'She's gone to Oxford Street with Mum. They're Luddites – I tried to explain that you can buy things on the in-ter-net but . . .' He shrugged.

It was a treat to have him to myself. We sat on the bridge at the bottom of Meadow Walk eating 99s, and I told him all about my trip.

'It's like going back in time . . . They have nothing, except fields and cows and —'

'What? No Wi-Fi?' he said. 'Inhuman.'

'There's no such thing as grabbing a snack, like beans on toast. Seriously, we made every meal from scratch and ate in groups of ten or —'

'Sounds like feeding time at the zoo.'

'They do *everything* by hand.'

As his comments got more barbed – 'It sounds very primitive, Samiya' – my monologue trailed off . . .

'It's not a crime to live in a poor country, Hugo.'

'No, but it's a bore.' He stood up and chucked the remains of his cone at an unsuspecting duck. 'Do you want to come to the house?'

Despite him being so dismissive of the whole finding-my-roots story, I was still keen to see where he lived.

'OK.'

'We'll get a taxi,' he said, scrolling down his contacts to T.

The driver dropped us in front of a modern house, all glass and wood. There was a Range Rover in the drive.

'Is your dad here?'

'No. He's hardly ever here.'

The hall had a mirror on one wall that was way taller than either of us. I stopped in front of it. Hugo was wearing skinny jeans, pointed black boots and a stripy T-shirt – sort of French-looking. My outfit was more Primark.

He winked at me in the mirror and then turned his face and kissed me. It was totally unexpected, and a hundred per cent deliriously brilliant.

He took my hand and led me upstairs to 'watch a movie'.

Hugo's bedroom had a black squishy sofa, two computers on a glass desk and a bed bigger than my mum and dad's. He pulled me onto it.

Close up, he was alarmingly hairless. I looked positively furry in comparison.

My dad always said boys were only after one thing, never contemplating the idea that girls might be after the same thing. What happened next was down to the both of us.

We were sharing a pillow, mid-chat, when Hugo reached across to get his iPad and held it above our two heads to take a selfie.

I put my hand in the way – photos always reminded me of how brown I was compared to my lily-white friends – but I was too late.

'We look good,' he said, showing me. 'Like a chocolate éclair.'

He was right – we did look good.

I went into his en-suite bathroom and tidied myself up. When I came out he was sitting at his desk.

'Mum'll be home soon,' he said, swivelling round. 'Might be better if you're not here. We have *trust* issues.'

I made a quizzical face.

'One of the many downsides of being expelled from school.'

'What did you do?'

'We had a sort of rave . . .'

'Tell me.'

He sighed.

'Dad was away and Mum couldn't be bothered to come and get us, so Juliette and I had to stay in the boarding house for the weekend, and some of our friends stayed too and . . . it got out of hand.'

'How out of hand?

'Quite. We knew we were dead, so we barricaded ourselves in.'

'Did the police come?'

'In droves.'

'So that's why you arrived mid-GCSEs.'

'It is.'

Hugo kissed me and then manoeuvred me towards the stairs, clearly worried his mum would put a curse on me.

He offered to call a taxi but I only had three quid and didn't want to ask him for money, so I texted

Mum, gave her the twins' address and said I'd be outside – not keen for her to meet Hugo right at that moment.

Mums have antennae. As soon as I got in the car, she said, 'I think you'd better tell me what you've been up to, Samiya.'

She didn't really mean that. No one would want their daughter to describe *exactly* what they'd been up to.

'I haven't been *up to* anything.'

I got the raised-eyebrow look, so I told her the bare minimum.

'His name's Hugo. He's an undernourished albino. We're close.'

'Invite him round and we'll feed him up,' she said.

I did invite him round, but he only came to the house once – the next Wednesday, which was one of the days Mum worked at the art shop, so she didn't meet him. He didn't suggest I go to his again.

Despite my high hopes for the summer, I spent most of August at home on my own, reading and watching films. Lucy had started going out with Jake – the class comedian – and in no time they were inseparable. I did meet Hugo in Buckingham a few times but he had Juliette in tow, which was a bit annoying, though not unexpected. The twins were Loyal to each other, capital L. And quite happy to be hermits.

One afternoon, fed up with obsessing over whether Hugo and I were actually a couple, I decamped to the supermarket to find the ingredients my grandma had used – the goat became chicken – and surprised Mum and Dad with a Yemeni stew. It was the start of a cooking frenzy. I made breads, a biryani-type dish, samosas and green chutney, all from memory. The neighbours, Dad's footie mates and Mum's Zumba crowd all benefitted from my reincarnation as *chef extraordinaire*.

The day after we got our GCSE results, the twins left for Vancouver. Hugo was silent apart from three Snapchats – his big toe, Juliette coming out of American Eagle with three brown shopping bags and a seagull. I missed him, apart from when I was playing *EVE* on my new laptop (a reward for my stack of A*s), when I didn't think about anything at all.

Unlike the rest of us, who were wearing Marks & Spencer's suits 'because they're washable', Hugo and Juliette turned up on the first day of sixth form looking like models from *Vogue*. I only saw them briefly because we were put in different forms, but they waited for me after school.

Hugo kissed me on the lips.

'You're lucky I'm still here,' he said. 'I nearly got packed off to boarding school again for getting so many Bs.'

'He's promised to work hard,' said Juliette, with a disbelieving face.

'You'll help me, won't you, Samiya?'

'Maybe . . . if you grovel.'

Hugo dropped to his knees.

I stayed with them until their lift came, then headed home, happy, full of the future. My grades were good enough to do whatever I wanted – law, or maybe psychology. I had a boyfriend, of sorts. And since our trip to Yemen, I had a whole other bit of me to think about.

Dad's car was outside even though it was only five o'clock. I noticed, but didn't think anything of it. I let myself in, shouted, 'I'm home!' and headed straight for the kitchen as usual.

'In here, Samiya,' said Mum. Her voice was odd. I walked into the front room, knowing something was up.

My dad was crying. Proper body-shuddering sobbing. My big, strong dad with the neat moustache never cried.

Mum was sitting on the sofa next to him, puffy-eyed, her arm round his shoulders. She'd made a mascara river, which she tried to wipe away.

'What is it?' I said. I had that sensation in my stomach, like falling, even though I didn't know what was going on. *Cancer?*

'What's wrong?'

Mum looked across at Dad. He tried to tell me, but I couldn't follow him. He was so distraught. In between words, he gasped, rocked and held his head in his hands.

What I thought he might be saying refused to go in.

'Mum?'

'Come here, Samiya.'

She held my hands between hers and explained, choking on every other word, that an American drone had killed *Jaddah*. The idea that she was dead took hold, but I still couldn't understand how.

I'd heard Dad talking about drones, but we didn't see one the whole time we were in Yemen. I thought they flew over terrorist training camps, not villages.

'Did it crash?'

Mum looked at Dad.

'What happened?' I said.

Dad raised his head to look at me.

'It fired at her, Samiya.'

He howled.

'Shot?' I shouted.

'Nothing even to wash and bury!' wailed Dad.

'The drone fired a missile at her,' said Mum. 'She was in the fields.'

My knowledge of weapons was limited, but I knew a missile was huge. My grandma was tiny, bird-like.

I retched.

'Why?' I asked. 'Why?'

'A mistake,' said Mum. She hesitated, about to say something else.

'What?'

'It wasn't . . . only your grandma, Samiya.'

I knew.
I knew before she said the first letter.
My Lamyah too.

5

I slept, but almost wished I hadn't, because waking up
was like hearing the news all over again. I came downstairs in my pyjamas, expecting life to have changed,
expecting . . . I don't know, representatives from the
foreign office to come calling, or at the very least a
family summit, but no . . . Dad was heading out of the
door, eyes all bloodshot, but otherwise like it was a
normal day.

'Shouldn't you be . . . in mourning or something?'

'Nothing to be done, Samiya.'

He kissed Mum, hugged me and went off to work.

'Life has to go on,' she said, seeing my incredulous
face. 'If we all keep busy it'll help —'

'We're not bloody bees,' I said.

She started twisting the tea towel she was holding.

'I don't know what to say for the best, Samiya.
Except that we're all hurting.'

'Try being angry,' I said. 'And before you ask, no, I'm
not going to school.'

I went back to bed, but was too wired to just lie
there, so I started Googling. Anything was better than
picturing how it might have happened, wondering if

they'd had a chance to be scared, imagining what was left of them. In no time I was totally clued up on drones, aka UAVs – unmanned aerial vehicles – and their role in the war between America and the areas of the world they believed were rife with terrorists – basically Pakistan, Yemen and Afghanistan. More shocking than the idea that the Americans had flying robots, tooled up like Terminator, was the number of innocent casualties. Reports varied wildly, but the consensus was that they killed more goodies than baddies. I printed out a newspaper article that said American drones had killed 874 people in Pakistan, including 142 children, in their search for 24 named men. How could that be right?

At about ten, Mum came upstairs with a cup of tea and two pieces of toast.

'I've got to go to work, Samiya,' she said.

'Whatever.'

The accounts of the damage inflicted by Hellfire missiles – the Americans' weapon of choice – were chilling. My relatives weren't just murdered, they were vaporised. Here one minute, gone the next. A direct hit meant that nothing, literally nothing, survived.

I read story after story –

a whole wedding party mown down while travelling in convoy

an imam known for preaching peace to wayward jihadists, flattened outside his home

a journalist, who chose to dress the same as the

locals, slaughtered along with the rebels he was reporting on

– all killed by pilots whose feet stayed firmly on American soil.

There should have been a law about at least being in the same country as your target. If you never saw the blood, heard the screams or scraped up the flesh then did you really feel like you'd killed anybody?

I pictured some guy called Brad or Hank, sitting in the operations centre in the Nevada desert, drinking a supersize Starbucks and thinking about baseball, thumb on the trigger of a killing machine.

Not so different from playing Xbox, firing away on a plastic controller.

Bang! Bang! Dead.

6

I wanted to wear black and wail. I wanted the school to have a special assembly, like when our English teacher died. I wanted there to be a mountain of plastic-wrapped flowers outside our door. I wanted sympathy cards to pour through the letterbox like Harry Potter's invitations to wizard school. I wanted my dad to chain himself to some railings somewhere, not toddle off to work. I wanted to find someone who felt like I did. I wanted Hugo to make me feel better, not worse.

'Come on, Samiya, give it a rest,' he said.

'It's only been six days. Don't you have any idea how upsetting this is?'

'Not really,' he said.

We were in Buckingham, eating toasted teacakes in the café. Or at least, he was eating – I was talking.

'No one will even acknowledge there's been a wrongdoing. Yet it's clearly a war crime. Someone should be arrested and tried in The Hague.'

'And hanged,' said Hugo, tilting his head sideways to demonstrate.

'I read a blog by someone whose uncle's whole

village in Waziristan was razed to the ground with no apology, not a squeak in compensation —'

'That reliable source of information – *the blog*.'

I ignored him.

'There are internationally agreed rules about the use of biological, chemical and nuclear weapons, but not drones. I've written an email and a letter to the Prime Minister and our MP – he's a Tory – asking why that is.'

I watched him eat the last mouthful of *my* teacake.

'Good luck with that, Samiya. Got to go.'

I left too, but didn't go home. At home, Mum would be making tea and then Dad would come in from football training and everything would carry on as normal. That was their way of coping, but not mine. Instead, I walked. Ending up in the next village. I went round the back of the church to the graveyard, sat on a headstone and cried.

The vicar saw me from the window of his kitchen, he said, and came to see if I was all right.

'You can tell me to go away if you like.'

I shrugged. I didn't want the God squad hassling me, but, for once, being on my own wasn't working either.

'What's the point?' I said.

'It's not always clear,' he said. He was wearing cords and a checked shirt, and had a tanned face. More like a landscape gardener than a Bible-basher.

'If there was any justice in the world, bad things would get punished and good things rewarded,' I said.

'That does happen,' he said, 'but not in every instance.'

'Someone killed my grandma and my cousin,' I said. 'A pilot, flying a drone. He fired a missile at them.' The vicar didn't say anything, so I carried on. 'The video on a drone's really basic – not clear enough to spot whether something's a weapon or . . . a spade – and it's usually too far away anyway. You can probably tell if someone's white or brown, but you wouldn't be able to say whether it was Osama or Obama. A direct hit incinerates you. If you're further away, it might do something like blow your legs off, so you bleed to death slowly. I don't know how my relatives died. No one does.'

'I'm very sorry.'

'Is that all you can think of to say?'

'No. But it's all I dare say at the moment, because I can see you're upset.'

He was quite likeable. At least he didn't say *she is at peace* or *the Lord has her in his warm embrace*. So I told the story, in full. He listened, nodding every so often, and then gave me a lift home.

'Thank you,' I said, and I meant it. He'd been a lot kinder than almost everyone else.

'My sympathies to your family,' he said as I got out. And then he blew it.

'Your grandmother and your cousin – they are both at peace now.'

Total and utter rot. They weren't at peace. They were in bits.

7

It was like being in one of those dreams where you need to catch a train but no one will tell you where the station is and when you eventually get to the station the doors of the train are all locked and when you ask the conductor he speaks a language you've never heard so you bang on the windows but no one can hear you. Except in a dream you get to wake up.

I emailed the Prime Minister again, copied to the Minister of State for the Armed Forces, and when I got no joy, I tried the US President, several senators who had denounced the drone wars and the Chief of Staff of the US Army, asking for information about the military operation. In return I received two condolence notes. Big deal. I made an appointment to see my MP, who was short (in height) and short with me. You could tell from the cracks in the skin of his fingertips that he was a gardener, but when I tried to suggest he had something in common with my grandma he was quick to close down the small talk, repeating, 'The American Military insist the strike was based on intelligence that a known insurgent was in the area.' I asked for the name of the known insurgent. Classified.

I made a file of all missile attacks involving civilians, collecting names and dates, comparing the reports of each incident and plotting the locations using a mapping app. I kept a tally of deaths.

I bookmarked anti-drone bloggers and joined all the human rights groups that had drones on their agenda.

But none of these things changed anything. There was no acknowledgement, no explanation, no apology.

There was hardly any acknowledgement at home either. I could tell that Mum and Dad talked about it on their own – I'd find them standing close together, glassy-eyed, connected somehow – but when we were together the only one who mentioned the elephant in the room was me.

I had the best conversations about my 'truth and reconciliation' mission with Lucy, but she was often wrapped up, literally, with Jake. I could hardly blame her for not dropping everything in my hour of need, given the way I'd pretty much dropped her for Hugo. *He* was useless, declaring the whole subject 'boring'. Dullness was a sin in his book.

Everyone else at school found it hard to know what to say – having your Yemeni relatives murdered by the US Military was Awkward, capital A, given that America was our ally and the home of Nike and Converse, and Yemen was full of men in dresses – so they mostly said nothing.

Although behind my back it was a different story.

I was in the corridor outside the sixth-form common room – three and a half weeks after the drone strike – when I heard Hugo say, 'I'd put money on Samiya's granny being the head of a terrorist cell.'

I couldn't believe what I was hearing. Or what he said next.

'I have it on good authority that "in the fields" is a euphemism for "jihadi training camp".'

There was tentative laughter, which stopped dead as I walked in.

'What was that you were saying?' I asked. I was calm, but inside the rage that had been there since what the Americans called 'collateral damage' but I called murder, was white hot.

'We were just having a joke, Samiya.'

'You'll have to help me, Hugo. I can't see the funny side.'

He was ever so slightly thrown – a rare thing.

But his response, slow in coming, was far from apologetic.

'I'm sorry, truly I am, but face it – who does most of the blowing up?' He paused for effect, hands outstretched to imply trust. 'Americans . . . or Muslims?'

'You wouldn't be confusing jihadis with Muslims, would you?' I said. 'Because only a very ignorant person would do that.'

The whole common room piled in, suddenly sure which side they were on.

'Suicide bombers are no more representative of Islam than the IRA are of Catholicism,' said Niamh.

'Xenophobic crap,' said Tom.

'It's your kind of attitude that starts wars,' said Caitlin.

'You're confusing faith with fanaticism,' said Ollie, which was a nice bit of alliteration.

At one point, Hugo tried to defend his statement.

'Yemen is rife with terrorists. I'm sure Samiya's grandma wasn't one, but half the village undoubtedly was.'

He was showing the side of his character better kept in the shadows. The side that would do whatever it took to get a rise from the audience. Even if it meant hurting someone he was close to . . .

Gradually the room emptied, leaving just the twins and me.

'No hard feelings,' said Hugo. 'Good to get everyone wound up every so often. And they were all rooting for the Mohammeds . . .'

He smiled at his own wit.

I smiled too, as though agreeing, took my hand back and slapped him so hard his head spun round. Juliette rushed to his side.

'Stay away from us,' she said.

'My pleasure,' I said. I walked off, normal pace, head high, broken inside.

I couldn't stay at school after such a public betrayal, but didn't want to go home. So I wandered down the road to town. I passed the bus stop just as the X60 was pulling up, on its way to Aylesbury. I hadn't been there since our class went on a trip to the mosque. I wasn't a Muslim, but everyone in my dad's village was. I turned round and joined the queue to get on.

8

I didn't need to ask the way, just had to keep an eye on the tall white minaret.

As I got nearer, I began to wonder quite what I was going to do when I got there. I couldn't talk to anyone religious wearing a short, tight black skirt with the slit ripped . . . But I carried on anyway.

There was an indecipherable hum coming from inside the mosque, but the street was quiet. I sat on a wall opposite and waited, trying to remember the names of the five prayer times – Fajr, Zuhr, Asr, Maghrib, Isha.

Although Dad grew up a Muslim, he left it behind when he came to England. I wondered whether, if he'd kept his faith, I'd have shown more interest, begged to visit his family, had a different life . . .

The hordes of men pouring out of the mosque interrupted my thoughts. They were a mixed bunch, some walking briskly as though they were late, some dawdling. Lots were wearing normal western clothes, but plenty had on thobes. There were hats and bare heads, crew-cuts and huge bushy beards. Women followed, some hijabed, some in abayas, but no one with their whole face covered in a niqab. The babble, much of it in a language I couldn't understand, reminded me of being in Dad's village. It was, at the same time, comforting and distressing. As they trooped past, I tried not to notice the girl with the white hijab who walked a bit like Lamyah, or the old ladies, swathed in black.

The idea that I might find some kind of answer in a religion I didn't believe in slipped away. The deaths had nothing to do with faith. And everything to do with the Americans' so-called 'Kill List' of militants they wanted to assassinate. Anyone who got in the way was fair game.

As the crowd thinned, leaving only a couple of stragglers, the muddle in my head started to clear too. Being angry, hating Hugo, the exasperation with my parents – all those feelings weren't helping. I needed to use logic – a far more useful tool than rage or hurt – to find a way to move on.

Hugo's words weren't important – he was being deliberately provocative (and despicable and damaged) – but what lay behind them was. *I* knew that the Americans had fired at the wrong target, but the world wasn't so sure. There was a cloud of suspicion, fuelled by the constant talk of Yemen being a hotbed for jihadis. If I could find out who the airstrike had intended to obliterate that day, I could prove that the pilot had made an error and demand an apology. Unlike most of the victims' families, I wasn't living in a hillside village without a way to make myself heard. I was educated. I was British. And thanks to social media and the internet, I had access to everyone and everything. My personal story could propel the issue of civilian deaths onto the front page. I remembered telling Dad – a few days after the drone strike, when I was still hoping he might take a stand – that the United Nations had declared the level of civilian casualties as a result of drone strikes 'both too high and not transparent enough'. I needed to be part of that growing indignation. I needed to stoke the fire. It was time to stop asking for help, and help myself.

And Hugo . . . I wouldn't make that mistake again. I'd let my infatuation with him obscure what was in front of me all along. Hugo had never cared about me. I amused him, and I guess he fancied me. End of.

Walking back to the bus stop, I felt a bit better. More grounded. I had a sense that I'd been like a runaway kite, tossed about by gusts, only just managing not to crash, but now my string was tethered, snagged on a branch, leaving me slightly less vulnerable to the changes of the wind.

9

I tweeted every day – pasting links to reports of airstrikes and asking the US and British governments for answers – and replied to any #drones tweets. My followers steadily grew in number (TFTF @voucherworld and @temptingtoys). I wrote blogs trying all sorts of angles, from an open letter to Obama to a description of my trip to Yemen and the aftermath. I shared other bloggers' posts and they shared mine. I peppered Facebook with drone-related statuses, which got Likes – although not as many as the cat that could play the piano. I started an online petition, which a sympathetic hacker I came across in a chatroom kindly populated with signatures. Letters to the newspapers, comments on other people's articles – you name it, I did it.

It felt better to have a purpose, but did nothing for my relationship with Mum and Dad. I knew Dad was devastated, but the way he calmly carried on with the same life we'd had before the disaster was hard to fathom.

'We can't bring them back, Samiya,' was his standard line.

I wasn't asking him to fly to the White House, but

he could have started an action group, gone on a march, put a poster in the flipping window . . .

Sometimes, I felt like a stranger in my own family. People at school were starting to talk about universities – for me, it couldn't come soon enough.

When doubt that I could change anything overwhelmed me, I'd take out my most precious photo. Three grins – me, Lamyah and *Jaddah*. It was too cruel. *Jaddah* was old by Yemeni standards, but Lamyah was my age. She could have been a neurosurgeon, or worked for the United Nations . . . We could have gone to Harvard together . . .

It was better not to dwell on what could have been.

In between making a noise on social media, I spent more and more time in chatrooms. OK, they're full of lunatics, but the way I saw things, it was lunacy to ignore murder. My family were the mad ones. I was sane.

I chatted to hackers, psychos, Jedis, Christians, fruitarians . . . Seriously, I mouthed off to everyone, looking for a way to hold the US to account. It was time-consuming, but I kept up with schoolwork – I had no intention of going to a second-rate university. What went by the wayside was gaming, although I occasionally shot folks on *Call of Duty* for a bit of R&R.

Sayge first appeared on a dull day in January, the day before the new term. I was looking forward to going back to school, because Christmas had been suffocating.

All fake cheeriness. Lucy had been skiing in the Alps with Jake's family, so I'd been pretty solitary, not that I minded that – it was the stream of jolly visitors that had grated. I'd have preferred to ignore Christmas, out of respect for the two members of our family who would never celebrate anything again.

I was trawling through the usual sites when Reuters broke the news of an airstrike in Pakistan that had killed a family of five. I wrote:

wonder what the coverage would be like if an American family of five had been slaughtered

– because you can say anything you like on the internet.

Sayge typed:

be more careful about what you say or use another name

I don't care – I haven't done anything wrong

– I replied.

not yet – he typed.

I'm the victim – not the aggressor

explain

I did. Pointing out that it was *because* I was the granddaughter and cousin of two dead Yemenis that I was there, so why hide my name?

After that, he started to pop up everywhere.

Sayge had no clear political or religious agenda. But he seemed keen on trouble. And keen on chatting to me. He said change was only brought about by force, quoting someone called Frederick Douglass *a lot* –

you can't have the ocean without the roar
you can't have the crops without ploughing
I looked him up online.

He was an escaped slave who became a campaigner, committed to using words not violence, until he reluctantly realised that 'agitation', as he called it, was a necessity because people with power never hand it over willingly. Some people call him the father of the civil rights movement, but back then he was a scary black guy upsetting all the white landowners.

The more my pleas on social media went unanswered, the more what Sayge had to say made sense. He had example after example of good people who'd done bad things for good reasons:

Mandela tried the courts but it didn't work – the ANC bombed their way to power

even the suffragettes – nice ladies in long skirts – became arsonists and bombers because no one would listen

I knew that feeling.

Sayge had a knack of hitting on exactly what was on my mind. The more we chatted, the more I liked him. He was my alter ego.

10

I went in search of Sayge after school one particularly bad Monday.

It started with some army chap on the radio being all gung-ho about a successful *British* missile strike that was targeting militants but probably killed all sorts of law-abiding bakers, tailors and candlestick-makers. The interviewer didn't make him define 'success'. I tweeted to that effect, with a link to the BBC. Then, joy of joy, first period was maths with the twins, neither of whom I'd spoken to since the slap. Our teacher, Mrs Abrahms, asked Hugo and I to stay behind.

'I need some help with the Junior Mentoring Club and was hoping you two might do it. Tuesday lunch-times. What do you think?'

'That's fine by me,' said Hugo.

'It'll be an excellent thing to write on your personal statement,' she said, looking at me. 'University applications come round in no time.'

'Sorry,' I said.

She waited for my excuse. Anything would have done, but . . .

'I can't bear to be anywhere near him, I'm afraid.'

I left, cross with myself for letting Hugo see that I was still bruised. Worse still, Mrs Abrahms came to find me later, 'concerned', and keen for me to see the school counsellor.

I told Sayge all about it.

I don't need a shrink – I need to put a missile up America – I typed.

if GCHQ are any good they're watching you

He suggested we meet in our own IRC channel where no one could listen in. Sounded good to me, whatever it was.

Away from the eyes and ears of the security services, he asked:

How would you get back at the Americans if you could do anything?

I'd find the guy who did it and vaporise his whole family – I typed.

I didn't mean it. Or at least, I didn't bother to think about whether I did or not.

I asked him the same. His answers were stupid.

Nail Obama on the cross

Nuke Washington

Pump nerve gas into the subway

But it was the start of a game. The sort of game that would get you in front of a judge accused of inciting violence, but a game just the same.

I'd always been good at picking things up – plotting revenge attacks was no different. I researched ways around security procedures at airports and the pros and cons of petrol, pipe, nail and pressure-cooker bombs. I watched YouTube videos showing how to make a remote detonator and, by accident, a cake in the shape of a grenade. One day I bunked off school and by the time Sayge came online at six I'd become a firearms expert.

We pretended to be snipers with a mission to take down a US senator, working through the stages from recces of targets to choice of ammo and getaway car. We orchestrated a lethal-gas attack on the New York subway, poisoned the President's food on Air Force One and took a whole army base hostage. It was harmless, but intensely satisfying.

I didn't see it coming, but wasn't surprised, when Sayge asked:

would you kill innocent people to get your own back?

I didn't reply immediately. I knew I was *meant* to say that I wouldn't . . . but my grandma was an innocent person, murdered not by a lone maniac, which would be sad but bearable, but by the world's greatest super-power.

well? – Sayge typed.

Jaddah and Lamyah were collateral damage. Only by making collateral damage of my own would anyone take any notice. Like Frederick Douglass said, there had to be a cost or nothing would change.

if by killing some random Americans I could

**guarantee the drone wars would stop – YES – I'd
do it**

   good – he typed.

I don't know if making a statement to a stranger in a chatroom marked the moment I considered becoming a bona fide activist. After all, they were just words. I do know that Sayge made it his business to encourage me.

**the drone wars will carry on unless the Americans
are forced to stop**

**only someone personally affected cares enough
to force the change**

you are that person

He helped me understand that it only took one person to start a whole movement. Made me realise that the person who feels the injustice most is the one who finds a way to stop it. History had example after example of individuals who fought back against a more powerful enemy, and great things followed – slavery was abolished, women got the vote, the white South African government was overturned.

I'd tried asking for help . . . I'd tried raising the profile of the drone wars . . . Direct action was the next logical step.

I drifted off to sleep at night, fantasising about putting together an act of retribution that would make the world stop and stare in shock. Although many people would condemn me, there would be others who would applaud my determination to shame the pilots who fired the missiles, and the ones who ordered them to be fired. The military's increasing use of drones had enemies as well as fans. I loved the idea of taking a stand and having a whole load of strangers with weird usernames support my cause.

We stopped saying *if*, and started saying *when*.

11

The shops in Buckingham were rubbish, and I needed new jeans, so I got the bus to Milton Keynes. Mum offered to drive me but I didn't want to have to go for lunch and be chummy, so I lied and said I was going with Lucy. It was the Sunday after my seventeenth birthday, 4th February, aka Rosa Parks Day. Rosa Parks was on a bus when she was arrested for refusing to give her seat to a white man – she was 'coloured', which in Alabama in 1955 was on a par with being a dog. Her action that day sparked protests led by the one and only Martin Luther King – someone else Sayge liked to quote.

For years now, I have heard the word 'wait'. This 'wait' has almost always meant 'never'.

I hoped, with all my heart, that for me the wait was nearly over.

I bought two pairs of jeans in New Look, one black, one grey. By one thirty I was done but in no hurry to go home, so I went to a café and bought a hot chocolate and a brownie. Sugar overload.

I chose a table by the window – always interested

in people-watching. The teenage boy in a huff, the kid in the pushchair swaddled in too many layers, the fashion-obsessed shopper strutting in high heels.

'Is this chair free?'

I looked up and nodded at the much younger version of my dad I'd noticed in the queue.

He dragged the chair to the table next to me, where he was joined by a friend – best guess, Pakistani. As they tucked into their cinnamon swirls, the conversation darted about from football to work to 4G. I kept an ear on them, and an eye on the window.

Someone had left a paper, which the Dad-lookalike started to flick through while his mate described his shift at the hospital – sounded like he was a nurse.

'Have you seen this?' said the Dad-lookalike.

He read the headline out loud.

'Anti-drone activists' anger at Obama's "kill" policy.'

I was pleased to see the story had been picked up by the newspapers. The protests had started in New York, and were moving to a different American city every day for the whole month of February. There was loads about the campaign online. But I hadn't heard anyone mention it until now . . .

'It won't make any difference,' said the nurse. 'The drones fly over Waziristan for hours and hours. The locals don't even look up – they're used to it. They know they can be shot at any moment. But what can they do?'

'A missile isn't like a gun, Amir. It's like a bomb.'

'I know. What right do the Americans have to even be there?'

'They're the ones that turn people into terrorists. Bullies, harassing people trying to go about their normal lives.'

'Someone should give them a taste of their own medicine. How would they like that?' said the nurse. 'If drones hovered over Washington.'

'Launching a missile at the Oval Office – that would bring it home to them for sure.' The lookalike laughed. 'Serve them right for killing people for being Muslims.'

Their words bounced around inside my head.

An eye for an eye. A tooth for a tooth. A drone attack for a drone attack. It was perfect.

They started talking about their plans for the rest of the day, but I didn't listen. I had plans of my own.

I arrived home, keen to get in front of my laptop, to find that Mum had chosen exactly that moment to try to rebuild our relationship.

'Samiya, I know things have been difficult since *Jaddah* and Lamyah were murdered.'

Finally she was using an appropriate word, rather than trying to make things better by saying 'lost' or 'passed'.

'Dad and I want you to know that we're proud of you . . . really we are. We know how hard you've tried to get justice.' She paused. I could see she was working up to something by the way she kept shifting her weight from foot to foot. I wondered if she was going to offer to help . . .

'But maybe it's time to let it go. All the blogging and everything. Maybe the best thing you can do for them is work hard and get a good degree.'

It's a terrible feeling to despise your mum, but I did. She was so feeble, when I needed her to be strong. So keen to jolly me along, when all I wanted was to see that she was upset, like I was. I may only have known *Jaddah* and Lamyah for six weeks of my sixteen years, but we'd formed a bond. I didn't want to 'let it go'.

'I'll think about it,' I said, because that was the quickest way to escape. Every truthful answer in my head would have caused a massive row.

'I'm going to have a bath. It's freezing out.'

As I tried to walk past, Mum reached out and gave me a hug – it felt as uncomfortable as the one I got from the Father Christmas in Milton Keynes shopping centre when I was seven.

While the water was running I found Sayge, desperate to share.

got a brilliant idea

go on

steal an American drone

is that even possible?

no idea – thought hackers could do pretty much anything

assuming it is – do what with it? – he asked.

fly it to somewhere it can do the most damage then fire its missiles – Washington?

Drones were the enemy – vehicles for killing without conscience. Drones should be the tool. America should be the target. It fitted.

He was, as expected, enthusiastic.

like it

But full of questions.

how far can they fly?

how much damage can they do?

how big are they?

can a hacker really do that?

About to find out – I typed, and logged out.

I knew all about drone strikes, but not that much about drones themselves. With my laptop propped up on a towel by the side of the bath, I had a long soak, Googling madly. By the time Mum called me for dinner my knowledge base was much improved.

Drones *were* hackable. The Iranians claimed to have stolen a US drone by breaking into its control system.

A stolen drone could stay hidden. Air traffic control wasn't designed to spot UAVs – they're small and slow compared to planes.

Drones could be piloted or pre-programmed to fly on autopilot.

Pilots were trained using video games. (Made me wonder whether they realised the victims couldn't respawn.)

Predator drones fly for up to forty-two hours.

I levered myself out of the water, threw on my pyjamas even though it was only six o'clock, and went to play happy families.

The conversation was a bit strained, but the lamb chops with mint sauce and thick salty gravy were delicious, as was the feeling that I had, at last, found a way to put right a wrong.

I went to school on Monday, but came home after lunch knowing Mum would be at work. Sayge didn't pop up until six o'clock, at which point I swamped him with information. He'd obviously been researching stuff too.

video feed would show if drone going on wrong course

if feed fails drone is meant to return to base — I typed.

could replace the video feed with fake footage to delay discovery of hijack — he suggested.

good job – time for drone to get well away — I replied.

we could issue a warning with a message about drone wars

I hadn't thought of that.

yes – need to get the maximum publicity

I was fired up by it all. If we announced we had a drone flying low over Washington, surely we could rely on journalists to do the rest? They'd dig up all the filth about missile strikes, and collateral murder would be the subject of every headline.

Flying Serial Killers

On the day itself, the man on the sidewalk would get to experience the same fear as they had in my grandma's village, and then, with drones top of the agenda – *bang!* The great U S of A would get the same medicine as Pakistan, Yemen, Afghanistan and Somalia – a flipping huge missile in their backyard.

People think that bombers, arsonists, murderers, bank robbers and the like are a different species, but I don't think they are. Successful bombers, arsonists, murderers and bank robbers are planners. *I* was a planner.

I took the preparation of my maiden political act more seriously than the organisers of the 2012 Olympics, even downloading an app used for project management. In free periods I worked in the library or went home, and every evening I buried myself in my room. Mum thought I was cramming to get into Cambridge.

I broke the plan down into a series of tasks – most of which we didn't have the skills for. That didn't worry me. As long as we kept our ultimate goal a secret, I didn't imagine it would be *too* hard to recruit some keen hackers to help out. It was nice to think of our project being crowdsourced.

My only worry was whether, out there in the community of grey and black hats, we'd manage to find *the one* that had the talent to hack a drone. Assuming we did, I was sure I'd find a way to persuade him . . . or her. All those years spent watching the kids at school to make sure I fitted in hadn't been wasted. If anyone could befriend an elite hacker and encourage him to show off, I could.

12

Three weeks after I first had the idea, Sayge and I met online to decide what to do next.

it's definitely doable with the right l33ts — messaged Sayge.

I agree — I typed.

time to start recruiting then — typed Sayge.

I didn't expect to have second thoughts. Having someone by my side, urging me on, albeit virtually, had made all the difference. Yet I suddenly got cold feet. The talk, the planning, visualising Washington in a panic with an armed drone circling overhead had made me feel alive . . . but it had never felt real.

There was a long interval — by online messaging standards — while I tried to work out what I was thinking. I wanted revenge. I understood the need for drastic action. But . . .

we could steal the drone – send a warning but not fire — I typed.

Sayge didn't like my sudden attack of conscience.

nothing will change unless we make it – remember frederick douglass and malcolm x — he typed.

**if I kill a grandma I'm as bad as them – threats
are enough** – I typed.

**if someone attacks you and you respond you
are not the same because they are the aggressor
– your move is self-defence**

but both sides have done wrong – I typed.

what exactly did your grandma do wrong?

**I meant jihadists and americans have both done
wrong** – me.

since when was this about world politics?

The online discussion carried on, with us both typing
at the same time so the replies made no sense.

**a drone strike on American soil will highlight
the complete injustice of the stealth war targeting
exclusively Muslim tribal communities** – he typed.

I ran out of things to say. He didn't –

**violence is a legitimate tool in the fight for
human rights**

He said there was one rule for western lives, and
another for non-western ones. He said that there
would only be a reaction if we vaporised a 'White
Anglo-Saxon Protestant'. Society has changed for the
better because of people willing to stand up and make
waves. My actions would make the world reconsider
its use of drones. Once the public appreciated the
true horror of the high-tech assassinations, the intol-
erable killing of innocents would be stopped and its
perpetrators brought to account.

It was a strange sensation. I was, in some ways,

already committed, and yet a fundamental part of me was reluctant. Maybe it was the speed – we'd pushed the idea over the top of the hill and now it was careering down the other side, out of control, the momentum all its own.

'Grub's up!' shouted Mum. For once I was delighted to be dragged away.

I need to think – I typed.

thinking won't help – nor will writing silly little letters to your MP

Something grated. It might only have been twelve words, but he could hardly have been more condescending. The tone rang a bell . . .

I read the words aloud.

I didn't remember mentioning the letter to my Tory MP to Sayge.

The ringing in my head got louder, blocking out everything else. It wasn't a bell – it was a church tower full of bells.

got to go – talk tomorrow – I typed.

I went offline.

If what I suspected was true, I'd been incredibly stupid.

13

I got up early to escape the voices in my head, smothered some toast with Nutella, then left the house, desperate for some air. I sat in the park and, for the nth time, went back over my relationship with Sayge –

Who was he?

Why was he so keen to help?

How had he so easily gained my trust?

The same answer satisfied all the questions.

He knew me. He knew what made me tick.

It was laughable – me, the arch-manipulator, had almost certainly been manipulated.

But I had to be sure.

When I got home, Mum was about to go and watch Dad play football – he hardly ever got selected for the reserves, so it was a *big* deal.

'Want to come?'

'OK,' I said, which surprised her.

The more you think, the less clear things become. I concentrated on the game, cringed when Mum shouted out helpful advice and talked to a man with a nice black Labrador who was standing next to us.

Dad's team won, 3–0. Mum took him to the pub to celebrate.

By the time I went online on Sunday I knew exactly what I had to do.

Just like the paper chase that led the runners along the tracks and under the tunnel in *The Railway Children*, I needed Sayge to follow my scraps, without realising where they were heading.

not sure a like-for-like attack will get the most sympathy – I typed.

If you could hear a sigh over Wi-Fi, I heard one.

you don't want sympathy – you want the damage drones do to be top of the agenda

but what if top of the agenda are the lives I end up taking? – I replied.

that's what will catapult drone strikes into the news – he typed.

what if I kill a child?

I waited to see if Sayge would outline an argument I'd heard before.

in war there are casualties – no one suggests world war 2 was bad because children died

but the right and wrong was clear – Hitler was a maniac

exactly – think of the greater good – this is not about individuals

it is – my grandma was an individual

detach yourself from the personal

what? – I knew what he meant, but I needed to see it in black and white.

think of it like vaccination – to protect the masses everyone has the measles jab – if the odd kid dies that doesn't mean the practice is wrong

the parents wouldn't agree

some deaths are justifiable

There was the proof. He even used the same words as he had way back in Year 11 when some of the girls had been stressing about the HPV injections.

I replied straight away so he didn't realise he'd messed up, even though what I wanted to do was never, ever have anything to do with him ever again. I signed off a few minutes later –

sorry – not ready – still thinking it through

– convinced he still believed he was anonymous.

I sat back in my chair, closed my eyes and double-checked my memory of Hugo holding court in registration. He'd decided to summarise the history of vaccination – repeating that it was for the 'greater good', even if healthy children died along the way.

'We have a societal responsibility,' he'd said, which went over most people's heads.

Someone drippy had said, 'Does that mean we could die because of a jab?'

'Of course. Some deaths are justifiable.'

Hugo's statement had caused a girly panic, which, I quite enjoyed at the time. The memory of how I fawned over him brought on an attack of self-loathing, heightening my rage. Tears fell, wetting my face and then my T-shirt. Only the most enormous self-control stopped me getting a taxi to his house so I could pour petrol through the letterbox, having made sure he was inside. It was excruciating to imagine his (and Juliette's?) reaction when I'd shared my idea for the drone strike. I was so earnest – he must have died laughing. The humiliation was complete and utter.

As the shock receded, I felt like I'd been dreaming. How could a seventeen-year-old girl expect to steal a drone, fly it and unleash a missile on a major city? It was madness. Which meant I was mad. Or maybe I was bipolar. Invincible one minute, and despairing the next.

I knew all along I wouldn't confront him. Unmasked, Hugo would turn it into a huge joke. He'd work his magical spin on the story, making me the half-Arab weirdo, plotting to murder innocent Americans, and him the hero, uncovering my plans. Better that I carried on pretending, which meant getting in contact.

It took a few days for me to overcome my revulsion, but then self-preservation got the better of me.

I was never going to go through with it – you knew that – I typed.

No I didn't – had you down as the real thing

I think you just wanted to see how far I'd go

Hugo was smart. He'd soon see there was no point in pushing it.

I think you have a legitimate reason to take direct action – he typed, clearly keen to reel me back in. I wasn't biting. I changed tack.

who are you anyway? – I bet you're a kid

doesn't matter who I am

whatever – listen it was fun but I've got exams – I typed.

how about we blow up the houses of parliament on Nov 5? – he asked.

how about we don't – I replied.

It was all good. The tone was jokey. We were, on the face of it, still friends.

I'd keep his secret, because that meant he'd keep mine.

14

It was six months since the drone strike, and all my efforts – legitimate and otherwise – had come to nothing. I went to school, played mindless games on my laptop and tortured myself by constantly trawling through the latest reports of drone strikes. The mainstream news sites rarely referred to civilian casualties, concentrating on the militant targets. Anti-drone bloggers from the States, and the handful of local sources, provided the best information.

Time drifted by, but, despite what people say, it didn't heal. A car accident, leukaemia, taking a tablet from a bad batch of Es even – those deaths might be the sort you get over, but positioning the cross hairs over the image of an old lady's head, watching her stoop to pick some tomatoes and firing . . .

Every single day I woke up angry.

'Have you revised for the physics test?' Lucy asked one day at lunch. It was April – the month of my grandma's birthday. She would have been sixty-two.

'Sort of.'

'How about I come round? Do it together.'

No one had been to my house in months.

'OK.'

Mum was delighted. She cooked sausages, with mashed potato, beetroot and beans.

'How's the family?' she asked.

'Getting smaller,' said Lucy. Her two older brothers were already at universities up north.

'I bet your mum misses the boys.'

'She does a Tesco shop for them every two weeks,' said Lucy. 'All ready-meals and biscuits. They'll never learn to cook!'

We all laughed.

After demolishing strawberries and cream, we went back to my room on a mission to nail electrons, waves and photons.

'You're so lucky,' said Lucy. 'You only have to look at something once and you've got it.'

'You mean like flu?' I said. 'Or an STD?'

Her brain did one of those leaps that you can see from the outside.

'What happened with Hugo?'

'You know – there was that thing in the common room.'

'He told me he'd apologised.'

'Big deal.'

'You know he never comes out any more. I haven't seen him at a party since Halloween.'

Too busy being someone else.

'Juliette says he's constantly on the computer in his room. She thinks he's depressed.'

'Lucy, I really don't care.'

And I didn't. But I wondered if she did . . .

'Has something happened between you and Jake?'

Jake had messed up big time – Instagrammed with his tongue in the wrong mouth. Lucy claimed she wasn't bothered.

'Do you want to go to Milton Keynes on Saturday?' she asked as she was leaving. 'I need Birkenstocks.'

'Nobody *needs* Birkenstocks,' I said.

Joint eye-roll.

Dad came home to find me watching *24 Hours in A&E*, with Mum ironing by my side. He sensed the change in atmosphere and offered to make us both a cup of tea – Dad in the kitchen, a rare thing.

'Yes, please,' we both said.

'And a biscuit, love,' added Mum.

It was a kind of turning point, at least on the surface.

I threw myself into studying, went to Prezzo with Lucy and a load of others to celebrate her seventeenth birthday, spent a weekend with Aunty Helen in Chester, got glandular fever, but still did well in my exams. Lucy and I went to three open days in June – Cambridge, Leeds and Exeter. In August we had a family holiday in Norfolk, and I went to the Edinburgh Festival for three days, again with Lucy. I wrote my personal statement and read the list of suggested books for applicants studying law, although I wasn't sure that was what I wanted to do.

Why study law – or anything else, in fact – in a world that was so flawed that you could get up every day, go to work, kill the wrong people, go home with your pay cheque, get up the next day and do the same thing, without ever being blamed?

The agonising was all rather pointless, because it wasn't meant to be.

Fate stepped in and showed me the way.

15

As the anniversary of the drone strike drew near I felt like a black cloud was weighing me down. On the day itself, I stayed in bed, reliving that terrible, terrible day –

Going to school in my M&S suit for the first time – a sixth-former at last. Being eager to see Hugo. The kiss after school. My cheerful walk home. Dad crying on the sofa . . .

I got scared of the emotion that was building, so I got up, unplugged my laptop and took it back to bed. One of the anti-drone bloggers I followed had posted a link to a YouTube video. I clicked. It was a boy from a remote village in Pakistan. He told the story of what had happened to him and his sister when they were picking okra in their fields with their grandmother the day before the festival of Eid.

He said a drone appeared out of the bright-blue sky, making the *dum-dum* noise, but he wasn't worried because only the three of them were there. Then the drone fired, making the ground shake and black poisonous smoke and dust fill the air. He ran, but the drone fired again.

'They always do,' he said, 'to kill the relatives who come to help.'

The second missile broke both his legs.

His sixty-seven-year-old grandmother, a midwife, was killed. He was taken to hospital, together with seven other members of his family, all injured by the shrapnel.

He held up an X-ray of his legs, showing the rods that had been put in to mend his shattered limbs.

His final, trembling words were: 'She was the heart of our village. My friends, they say we all lost a grandmother that day.'

The video swapped to show his sister. She gave her version, which was similar but more distressing, because I knew what was coming. Her big brown eyes, not dissimilar from my own, stared at me from the screen of my laptop. They were asking me to do something.

16

I made a pseudonym — a deliberately common one. And Angel (ANG3L for fun) was born. There was something nice about my alias having wings, given what I was up against.

It's crazy the way having a different identity frees you. I was everywhere, making friends with unsuspecting users on all sorts of forums, gathering information and building a network of contacts that might be useful. I got a second phone, because a guy from a protest group said he wanted to check I wasn't an informer but in fact wanted to say rude things to me. I took it all in my stride. My goal was clear. The drone wars needed to stop.

No matter what I came up with, nothing was as perfect as the plan Sayge and I had put together. And the more I thought about going ahead with it, the more certain I was that it was meant to be.

Fate had thrown Hugo and I together.

Fate had made me overhear the conversation in the café.

Fate had given me Sayge to help me devise the plan.

Fate had shown me when I no longer needed him.

Fate had sent me the faces of the little brother and sister.

(For fate, read Allah, luck, God, the zodiac, tarot, The Force – whatever suits.)

Obviously Hugo would realise it was me – what were the chances of another activist stumbling on the same idea? But if he told anyone, *he'd* be implicated big time. Knowing Hugo as I did, he was the last person to martyr himself for the greater good. And anyway, he wanted me to do it – like those weirdos on the web who goad people into committing suicide.

Deciding to go for it brought relief. It brought fear too, but fear meant adrenalin. And adrenalin was way better than procrastination.

Although my hacking was strictly script-kiddie level, I'd learnt enough jargon along the way to blend in with the elites. I'd always been good at adapting – immersing myself in the dark web was no different. I knew it would be a slow burn, but I'd waited a year. Time didn't matter. Success was what mattered.

Hackers turned out to be unexpectedly generous people. My first gift was a few simple mods of code to use when playing *Starcraft*, which meant no other players stood a chance. Soon after, someone magicked up a subscription to Netflix for me. Proof that I was making the right kind of friends.

I had a lesson in bots and how to use them to launch a DDoS attack, which basically paralyses a website, and saw a way to make the impact of my plan even greater. If, just as a drone flew over, the ticketing site for the subway happened to go down, there'd be the maximum number of people panicking on the street. Good job.

Angel quickly became a popular member of the online community. Making friends you couldn't actually eyeball was just as easy as making face-to-face friends – basic things like reflecting back their own opinions made people think I was like-minded. Being witty helped too.

As I roamed around, I was constantly on the lookout for *the* hacker who might have the capability to hijack a drone, and considering how best to coax him into helping when I eventually did.

I spent hours online, but still went to school, did my homework, talked to Mum and Dad, went out with Lucy (occasionally), ignored Hugo and Juliette and put in my UCAS application just before the October deadline for Oxbridge. If I was serious, which I was, I needed to blend in like everyone else – loners who withdrew from society got noticed.

Mum came with me to parents' evening, wearing a spotty dress and nice make-up. Dad was at football training, desperate to keep a place in the reserves despite hitting forty.

'As you know I've predicted you an A* – hard to come by in this subject,' said the head of English. Everyone else said more or less the same.

The last appointment was with my maths teacher, Mrs Abrahms, who'd written me a brilliant reference for Cambridge.

'The interview can be unpredictable, but I doubt Samiya will have a problem. Once she decides on a thing, I find there's no stopping her.'

Mum was bursting with pride, imagining me in legal robes and a wig, but I felt nothing. My future was to be a game-changer . . . a political activist . . . a rebel with a cause . . .

17

The plan got better as time went on, but it was still just a plan. My web of contacts got wider, but it was still just a pool of potential. The armed drones continued to invade from the skies with no come-back. It was agonising to watch the numbers of dead and injured grow, like Scrabble scores but with only one possible winner. But I had to wait, and keep the faith.

Often, when I was walking to school and back, I'd imagine a drone appearing from nowhere – a dark silhouette, flying low. It was my way of trying to feel the fear of the Pakistani children in the video, my way of staying connected. They said that they didn't go out in the sun any more because they were too frightened. Only when it was cloudy and the drones couldn't see would they go to school. They were by my side, together with every other family who had lost someone because of a grainy image on a screen.

Christmas came and went. I got offers to study law from all the universities I'd applied to, including Cambridge – despite a surreal interview about the alleged theft of a cat. Mum and Dad were over the moon, but I had a premonition that I wouldn't actually be going. January drizzled past, and suddenly it was my eighteenth birthday. Mum and Dad bought me twelve driving lessons. I pretended to be thrilled, but all I could think about was the fact that it was a whole year since I'd sat in that café in Milton Keynes, eavesdropping on the table next door. It felt as though the second anniversary of the deaths of *Jaddah* and Lamyah might slide by and I'd still be in limbo.

And then someone called KP – like the peanuts – came on the scene.

I met him playing *EVE*, and we got on immediately. So much so that a couple of battles later, he offered me free credit for my phone – he'd put together a neat bit of code and wanted to show me how cool it was. I sent him the number of my second phone and, hey presto, fifty quid.

He clearly wasn't bothered about stranger danger, letting slip his real name – Dan – and the fact that he was only sixteen.

He came online one evening in a bit of a state. His mate had been knocked off his bike by a white van, and Dan had just been to see him in hospital. It sounded quite bad. The driver didn't stop, which made the whole thing much worse. My destiny changed because of a random suggestion I made to help him get even.

hack the council security cameras – get the reg of the van – I typed

might just do that – he replied.

We carried on playing *EVE* and I didn't think any more about it. I was constantly dropping things into conversation, in the hope they'd lead somewhere, and being disappointed.

Two days later, Dan came to find me.

got the camera but not the crash

shame – me.

good idea tho – got a present for you to say thanks

Dan sent me the incredibly useful series of indecipherable commands that, like magic, turned into pounds of mobile credit. I was very grateful, and immediately started to sell it online at half-price, which turned into a nice little income stream via a PayPal account. One particularly busy day, I made two thousand quid thanks to word of mouth. Insane. I was so going to be the richest kid at university.

I decided Dan was a definite possibility – if that made sense. He knew his stuff, wasn't bothered about breaking the law and, bottom line, I had a good feeling about him. Of all my hacker friends, he was the one I had most fun with.

was it a long job? – I asked.

took 2 episodes QI – Dan measured life in episodes, not time. Quirky.

My instinct about him made me take the next step. He wanted to find the guilty driver who'd ploughed into his friend. I wanted to get inside the military. I saw an opportunity and went for it.

maybe try the spy satellite network – I typed.

All I thought about was whether my casual remark had spurred Dan into action. Every time we met online I was tempted to ask if he'd had a go, but made myself stick to the usual chat. He'd got my gender wrong, which I quite liked, because boys talk to boys in a different way. Equal.

A few times we both stayed off school and spent all day gaming. It was a calculated risk – bad for my quest to appear like a law-abiding member of the Upper Sixth, good for building up the trust between us. I got to know all about his mum, his kid sister – who I wished was my kid sister – his mates, where he went in Bristol and much more.

Although I was closest to Dan, I touched base with Annacando, Expendable and Omen II pretty much every day. They were mischief-makers, up for bringing down sites, hacking competitions, getting free stuff – but none of them were political. I worked hard to make sure I used the right language. They had to believe that I was like them.

My other regular contact was an American I found on a home video group. When the time came, he was going to make me a video to convince the UAV pilot that the drone had crashed, not been kidnapped. I'd told him I was doing film studies.

Guaranteed, they'd all have wet their pants if they'd had even an inkling of what I was really about.

The breakthrough came on a Friday. Dan and I were playing *GTA V* when he typed, with no warning, no 'guess what?':

infiltrated the US Military network

what? – I replied, hands trembling.

got in through a remote base station near Camp Bastion – found the satellite system

He was *so* casual. I was ecstatic, but just wrote:

great job

I asked a few questions. Three-quarters of his answers were incomprehensible, but that didn't matter. What I *did* understand was that he'd mapped the controls onto his iPhone to manipulate the live satellite feed.

Amazing – I typed.

I could see, at long last, that the theory could work. If you could hack the US Military satellite network, surely you could hack a drone – they weren't much more than cameras that moved to order.

Time to get serious.

I spent the whole of the next day waiting for Dan to show up. I had no appetite but forced a wrap down at lunchtime so Mum didn't fuss. The butterflies in my tummy were more like bats. I couldn't concentrate on anything.

Come on, Dan.

When I eventually found him playing *EVE*, we had a bit of banter about his geography trip at a residential centre in Wales, and then I suggested we meet at IRC channel #angeldust.

more private

I could tell he liked the idea.

Dan joined us on #angeldust to find we were planning a botnet. In fact, only two other members were real, the rest of the virtual gang were all me. It was a cute trick – being eight people at once. It meant I could guide the conversation.

this is a closed group – you are a guest – I typed.

OK – that was KP, aka Dan.

unless you pass a test – me.

we all had to do that – nearly got me arrested – me, as someone else.

are the 5000 bots my test? – typed Annacando.

I made it seem as though everyone had passed an initiation to become a bona fide member of #angeldust, but deliberately didn't issue one to Dan, although it was clear he'd have to do one. He obliged by asking:

Like what?

we'll have to come up with something – I typed.

Grooming is a slow process, if you do it right. I

couldn't just chuck in the idea of a drone. It had to come out in its own time. His expectation was that he'd have to hack something – that was enough to be getting on with.

18

Dan got himself a girlfriend! Bad timing as far as I was concerned, because he was much more interested in seeing her than playing with me. He still popped up online most nights, but not till late and not for long. There was another annoying thing in his life called GCSEs. I tried not to stress too much. When the moment was right, I'd bring up the initiation. In the meantime, as I was meant to be a boy, I pretended to fancy girly girls with skinny legs. He said I should go out with a flamingo and that I was shallow. His girl-friend, Ruby, bit her nails and wore sloppy jumpers. She sounded hideous, but what did I know?

'Do you want to come over later?' Lucy asked in physics, a couple of weeks after I first introduced Dan to IRC #angeldust.

'OK,' I said, because it was better than waiting for Dan *again*. Not that I'd wasted the time. I'd found an American community college that had a drone-simulation programme and a pathetic firewall. Thanks to a lot of late nights, I was a fully fledged UAV pilot – or would have been if anyone had known about me.

Lucy's mum was pleased to see me.

'Stay for supper, Samiya. The table's far too empty these days with the boys gone.'

I couldn't see any reason not to.

We talked universities.

'You'll be in your element at Cambridge,' she said. 'I remember meeting you when you were about eight and being astonished at how smart you were even then.'

'Thanks,' I said, wondering if my memory of how she'd quizzed me about my Yemeni roots wasn't entirely accurate.

'Lucy can't decide where to go,' she said.

'That's because they all sound the same.' Lucy tucked her straight brown hair behind her ear – it fell straight back onto her face. Mine had grown back into the non-style I used to have before my mission to be the same as everyone else.

'I still can't believe you're doing engineering, Lucy. You can't reliably refill a stapler,' I said. Her mum laughed.

'Luckily they don't ask for an A in use of stationery,' said Lucy.

'It'll be *all* boys,' I said.

'I hope so. If I don't get a good degree, at least I'll find a man with one.'

'Lucy!' Her mum pretended to be shocked.

They were more like friends. So different from Mum and me. Our house was like a B&B – all perfectly polite, but strictly business.

I got home at about eight to find that Mum and Dad had gone to the pub, like most Fridays. Dan came online at nine, live messaging on IRC as usual. There were only six of us – me, Dan, and four other mes with different names – because being eight people was too complicated. He started going on about how he'd watched rush hour in Tokyo using the spy satellites. I was immediately on high alert, hoping for an opening. Using one of my other usernames I asked:

what else have you spied on?

Dan was only too happy to supply a list that included the Great Wall of China and people leaving the Kremlin.

Various people commented – all me.

do something with it – don't just watch

like what? – that was Dan.

track a celebrity and sell the photo

catch a royal having an affair

spy on the US forces with their own cameras

hack a drone and fly it

could you do that KP? – I typed as Angel, praying he'd react.

if I wanted to be blacklisted by the most powerful country on the planet I could – Dan replied.

thats your challenge KP – hack a drone

I was convinced he wouldn't smell a rat. It sounded spontaneous, despite being anything but. Job done. Either he would. Or he wouldn't.

19

I had to be ready, just in case Dan came up with the goods.

The process of persuading my other online friends to provide the parts that would make the whole was already in motion, but I pressed the accelerator. Each one believed something different – a matrix reminded me what I'd told to who and when and why. I got in touch with them all.

As Friday night turned into Saturday morning, I heard Mum and Dad come back from the pub and their bedroom light go off. But America was still awake.

I'd been amassing bots for a while, but I needed more. Luckily, Annacando announced from her bedroom in Boston that she had 7,000 – not even bothering to ask why I wanted them. My other bot suppliers thought I was planning a DDoS on Amazon as a protest at their domination of all things bookish.

Next job was to approach my buddy with the video skills. He was only too happy to make me some FPV (first-person view – I used all the right jargon) video of a drone crashing. All he needed to know was what I wanted the terrain to look like. I said I'd get back to him.

Most of the other elements I needed were hidden away, virtually, like the code to take down the NBC TV website and replace the content with my own personal message to the American people, warning them that a drone was overhead. What I couldn't prepare in advance was the route for the drone to fly, because I didn't know where it would be starting from. However, I had an aviation geek ready to do that for me. I didn't know if my mapper was a man or a woman but, judging by the language, definitely a weirdo.

At five in the morning, I ran through the blueprint for my seek-and-destroy attack on Washington. There was nothing more I could do. It all rested on Dan. If he didn't take up the challenge, I was back to square one. I turned off my lamp, but that thought kept me awake.

On Saturday afternoon I started goading one of my other hacker friends to see where we went. We exchanged messages about famous hacks and then I jumped right in:

how hard is it to hack the national grid?
Why would you want to? – typed Omen II.
only asking out of intellectual curiosity – don't
stress
stick to gaming Angel – your out of your depth
(Omen II never could spell 'you're' correctly.)
thought you were a hacktivist – I typed.
Your body language gives away what you're really

thinking and, unbelievably, messaging can too. My attempt to steer the chat wasn't as subtle as I'd hoped.

stay away from me angel – your trouble

I left the game, cross with myself. I'd played a slow hand and then impatience had made me take a risk. I didn't need the word to go round that I was someone to avoid.

I worried on and off for the rest of the day.

On Sunday morning I couldn't be bothered to get out of bed. The chances of being able to help the Pakistani children whose faces haunted me were tiny. A drone would have so much more security surrounding it than a satellite camera. Dan was sixteen! It was all make-believe. If I really wanted to help I needed to do something like send a bomb to Obama . . .

Mum poked her head in when I didn't surface.

'I've brought you a cup of tea.'

'Thanks.'

'Your dad and I are off out for a walk.'

'OK.'

I sat up and took a huge glug of tea, then reached down and picked my laptop off the floor. Dan had been trying to find me in the worldwide wilderness.

meet me – he messaged.

I knew where to go.

He sent me some code that he said would put me in control of an American surveillance drone. He was totally matter-of-fact, not even hanging around to gloat.

challenge complete – got to go

It had to be a joke. I'd run the code and a birthday card would appear, or a message from EuroMillions saying I'd got the jackpot with no ticket. But I checked my already-shut bedroom door and closed my curtains anyway.

I executed the code.

After a few flashes of ASCII, my computer threw up a list. I cycled through a few of them, clicked one at random. My screen paused, then became a heads-up display, like when you're playing Xbox – an image overlaid with acronyms, numbers and lines. It was terrifying. I made myself study the data on the grid, jotting down the GPS co-ordinates, the speed and the altitude, before hitting Escape and snatching my fingers away from the keyboard as though they were burning.

Was it real?

I Googled everything I'd seen, cross-referencing. It all matched. The drone was in Djibouti, spying on Somalia presumably.

Dan had done it. He'd actually done it.

I resisted the urge to celebrate. There was one more hurdle.

I went back in and scanned the list, trying to understand how the drones were classified – I needed one with payload.

Sweat was pooling in my armpits. So close . . .

Or maybe not. They were *all* surveillance drones.

Use logic, Samiya.

I went back to the code. It was a series of commands – there had to be a clue. I scrolled through, slowly. Did it again. My eyes fixed on some adjacent letters that I'd seen before. I went back to the list of surveillance drones to check, and saw the same pattern. It was relatively easy, compared to the hard work Dan had done, to work out what to replace them with.

Holding my breath, I ran the code again. The new list was in red. I clicked. And took control of a Predator.

Fantasy finally became reality.

It was eighteen months and eighteen days since Brad or Hank, a bit bored by the four walls of his operations centre in the Nevada desert, had randomly pressed Fire, shattering my life and many others – some literally.

Time to settle the score.

20

I'd assumed the drone would be in America – which
was dim of me, as they don't bomb themselves – but
the co-ordinates from the Predator I'd temporarily
hijacked showed it was in Germany, on 'operations'.
So the first thing I had to do was rethink the plan.
Crossing the Atlantic wasn't feasible, but Germany was
only a hop away from England. Although their drone
activity was kept low-profile, the British were guilty
too. Quite cute to turn America's weapons on the
country that claimed they shared a 'special relationship'.

London was every bit as newsworthy as Washington.
It was a no-brainer. The botnet could disable London
Transport's ticketing service, the code to take down
NBC could do the same to the BBC, and the target
for the missile strike, well . . . there were plenty of
deserving locations in the capital.

Convinced it could work, I took the next logical
step, which was to disappear – not literally, virtually. I
abandoned IRC #angeldust and opened a new channel
that Dan would never find – IRC #paperchase. He'd
served his purpose, and any questions he might have
for me – like whether handing a drone over to a

complete stranger was a good idea – were definitely staying unanswered.

The adrenalin flooding my body combined with a lack of food put me off tackling the timing plan. I gave up and went to make a toasted sandwich and a cup of tea, which I took outside. Sitting on the patio in the sunshine, still wearing my pyjamas, I finally faced the inevitable.

The minute there was even a sniff of a drone being hacked or missing, Dan would know it was Angel and Hugo would know it was me. For all I knew, GCHQ were also on my tail – I'd certainly made enough noise to get on a watch list. Angel had been careful, but Samiya had left footprints belonging to yetis. Therefore, one way or another, I'd be caught.

So, assuming I didn't fancy life in prison, I had to leave home. It wasn't the first time I'd thought about it, but it had always been in the future . . .

I sat, staring at the sandwich, which was suddenly too hard to swallow. My brain wouldn't compute the pain I'd cause to Mum and Dad if I disappeared . . .

Or what it really meant . . .

Hiding in squats? Always moving on?

There was no point getting emotional – no one ever claimed that being an activist was easy. Either I took my A levels and went to Cambridge, or, I took a stand and spent the rest of my life looking over my shoulder.

I pretended to think it through, but there was only one answer.

When it first happened, Mum had said the murder of *Jaddah* and Lamyah was a mistake. If that had been the case, maybe I could have grieved and then slowly got over it. But that 'mistake' had been repeated again and again. It couldn't be allowed to go on. If I did nothing, nothing would change. That reminded me of another quote Sayge liked:

'All it takes for evil to triumph is for good people to do nothing.'

He might have been fake, but he was a good teacher.

The sun started to dip and a chill crept over the garden. I threw my sandwich in the wheelie bin and went back up to my room.

The only way I could steel myself to thrash out the timing plan that would take me one step closer was to think of it as homework. I made a list of tasks, put them in order of priority and then selected the ones that needed to happen at specific times before working backwards to determine how quickly I could put the plan into action. Even building in a couple of days of slack, two weeks was all I needed. I closed the file, terrified by how easy it all looked.

Mum and Dad came back and soon the smell of roast lamb started spiralling up the stairs.

I put the drone's GPS co-ordinates – taken from the HUD – into Google Maps and had a good look around, then emailed my video guy. I described the 'terrain', which was mostly German woodland – attaching some screen shots, and begged him to hurry so I didn't miss the deadline for my project. He promised to get me a video within the week.

Mum called me down before I could get started on the next job, which was a bit of a relief, because it was all moving way too fast.

21

For the next few days, I went to school, took my laptop, used a VPN tunnel to get past the firewall so I could do what I liked, came home and shut myself in my room.

Running away was a huge job. I had to think about the short term – laying low until after the missile strike – and the long term – a new identity.

According to the internet, there were two basic ways to reincarnate. Adopting the details of someone who'd died – undercover police liked to use dead babies – or being someone's double. Either way, the consensus was that with one good piece of ID, the rest, with patience, would fall into place.

I didn't use either method. Because someone else did it for me. I was too frightened of leaving a trace. Once Samiya had left Buckingham, the trail needed to be ice cold. As Angel, I bought a name, a copy of a birth certificate and a National Insurance number from an anonymous creature that inhabited the dark web. And then, because I couldn't imagine being called Georgia, I bought a second one. It was pricey, but I'd made thousands selling phone credit using Dan's hack – which sadly didn't work any more. Some cyber detective must have found the glitch.

The idea of hiding out in the holiday cottage we'd stayed at in Norfolk popped into my head with no warning – it was the perfect place. The lady who'd let us in when we arrived was a chatterbox, so I knew *all* about the 'foreign' owners. They'd bought it, done it up, and then decided it was too quiet and a nightmare to get to. That's Norfolk for you – stuck on the side. The property was advertised on Luxury Holiday Cottages Direct, so all I had to do was check the bookings page. Empty until May half-term. Couldn't be better.

Everything was falling into place. All that was left for me to decide was *when* I was leaving Buckingham. But that was the hardest thing of all. I was scared – something I found it hard to admit. So far, all I'd done was plot. If I took the next step, there'd be no going back.

Did I really want to be a fugitive for the rest of my life?

No, I didn't. But maybe it wouldn't turn out that way. Nelson Mandela, 'the black terrorist', ended up President of South Africa. Gerry Adams, who denied being an IRA operative, was photographed shaking hands with Tony Blair on the steps of Downing Street. Menachem Begin, aka Israel's former Prime Minister, blew up a hotel in Jerusalem, killing ninety-one people.

The path to political leadership wasn't necessarily Eton, then Oxford. The bomb-making route seemed just as effective.

Nothing to stop me being head of Liberty, having proved my dedication to human rights . . .

Fate decided me, like it did everything else.

I was in the library last period, four days after Dan sent me the code, when Hugo and Lucy turned up. Only she came over.

'You look busy,' she said.

I wanted to ask her why she was with Hugo, but I already knew the answer.

'English,' I said, with my arm over the book – the American civil rights movement wasn't on the syllabus.

'I'll leave you to it then,' she said. 'See you later.'

The two of them sat a few tables away and talked quietly.

I went back to staring at Malcolm X quotes.

'Usually when someone is sad, they don't do anything. They just cry over their condition. But when they get angry, they bring about a change.'

Critics of the black human rights activist said that the discriminatory laws would have been overturned without violence, but they didn't say when. And that's the critical bit – violent protest accelerates change. Throughout history, it's there again and again. You either wait for reformers to slowly change opinion, like the crawl towards women bishops, or you demand it.

The librarian didn't seem to be annoyed by Hugo and Lucy's whispering, but I was. It hurt to see their heads so close together, my only friend and my arch-enemy.

I turned the page.

'*By any means necessary,*' was Malcolm X's mantra. When white Americans accused him of condoning violence, he reminded them that his ancestors were brought to America in chains, kept in line by whipping, beaten to death for disobedience and torn apart by dogs for fun . . .

The side with the power can terrorise all they like, but only those who rise up against that power are called terrorists. White state troopers terrorised the black people who marched in Alabama asking for the vote. Drone pilots terrorise whole communities —

'Hi, Samiya.'

What the hell!

Hugo was standing right in front of me in his sharp suit. Lucy had disappeared.

'I've got nothing to say to you.'

He pulled out a chair and sat opposite me. Still beautiful.

'Lucy's idea,' he said. 'She thinks it's time we made up.'

I closed the book, collected my stuff together and stood up.

'I've said I'm sorry. You know me, like to play to the audience.'

He followed me along the corridor, speaking to my back.

'So did you ever get anywhere with all those letters to your MP?'

He was still trying to play with me, like a cat with a half-dead mouse.

'It's a shame,' he said, louder now, as I was further away. 'Someone should have done something.'

I galloped down the stairs, went into the girls' loos and sat on the seat with the door bolted – like a bullied teenager. A victim.

How sad was it that the only person who'd appeared to understand me was Sayge? And he wasn't real.

The tears ran down my face – I didn't bother to wipe them away.

Too much wallowing in self-pity makes you despise yourself. I had a wee, splashed water on my face in case Hugo was lurking and set off home.

Dad was at football. Mum was off out. As soon as she left, I went up into the loft to get the rucksack I used for my Duke of Edinburgh Award. When I'd packed the bare essentials, I left it in the lean-to out the back. I wrote an overly dramatic note saying I was going to stay with a girl I'd met at the Cambridge interviews because I needed 'some space'. I put it under my pillow, ready for the morning. Last of all, I committed social-media suicide, deleting all my accounts on everything.

There'd been altogether too much thinking.

First thing Friday, I was off.

22

Despite the enormity of what I was about to do, I made myself behave exactly as normal. The trick was not to think, just act. Quick goodbye to Dad, short conversation with Mum – without meeting her eye, school suit on – but soon to be replaced by jeans. Usual last-minute bolt up the stairs to fetch something I'd forgotten – this time it was the letter, which I put on my pillow.

I nipped round the back of the house, got my ruck-sack and walked to the roundabout, hoping no one I knew would see me before I got a lift. My wish was granted – as soon as I stuck out my thumb a red Golf stopped. It was a youngish bloke going to Bedford. Suited me. I told him I had an interview. Seemed more sensible than telling him I was on the run. Not that I intended to run anywhere. In all honesty, I wasn't sure what I was going to do. My horizon pretty much stopped at the date I'd chosen for London to go *kaboom!* My grandma's birthday – or thereabouts. Details like dates of birth, addresses, times were pretty fluid in the moun-tain village. Maybe I'd go back there . . . when it was all over.

As we joined the A5, he sped up. I had a sudden crazy death wish. If we crashed, I wouldn't have to be the one to take a stand. Mum and Dad could grieve for me and then carry on with their little lives. It would be easier all round . . .

Safely in Bedford, I changed out of my suit and dumped my phone – turned off, of course – in an industrial wheelie bin, so I couldn't be found using the GPS. I kept the one I'd bought when I became Angel in case I needed to make a call. I bought a panini and made myself eat it in the hope that it would settle my stomach – which it did.

The fear was there, but rather than crippling me, I felt alive.

The journey went better than I could have expected. A train to Cambridge, two more lifts, lots of small talk and a bus, and I was in Fakenham, Norfolk. I bought enough food for a couple of days and enough make-up for a beauty pageant, and then walked the half a mile along the lonely road to the house we'd stayed in. Not one car, tractor, van or bicycle passed me. A good omen.

I crept around the outside of the house first to make sure there hadn't been a last-minute booking. Nope. Deserted.

The code for the key safe hadn't changed. The alarm was off, as expected – the housekeeper had told me she didn't like messing with it.

I dumped my bags, checked the Wi-Fi was still connected – yes – and then collapsed on the sofa.

Mum and Dad wouldn't start to worry until Sunday evening, when I didn't arrive home. If they called the police, no one would do anything. Every year 140,000 teenagers go missing, that's 383 every day. I would be a statistic. Full stop. When they got round to making enquiries, people would mention my unsettled behaviour after the 'trouble' in Yemen. The Sherlock deduction would be that I'd run away. No one would think to mention a place we'd only been to once. I was safe for the moment. I'd given myself ten days, after which Samiya and Angel would both be history.

My true identity was bound to come out. If Hugo didn't betray me, the security services would eventually get there. I couldn't wait to see Samiya's life story in the headlines, making people understand why the drone wars had to stop. By that time I'd be using my alias, Saffron. Practising her life story by saying it out loud as I wandered around the house was a priority, as was creating her face.

I got into a little routine. Each morning I'd scrutinise a different part of the plan – paying particular attention to anything that could go wrong and making contingencies. After lunch I'd put on one of the ancient DVDs that were left in the house – because you can't think all the time. I watched *The Hunger Games* twice and *Love Actually* repeatedly.

For dinner I stuck to simple stuff because there was Nothing, capital N, in the kitchen, not even a flake of chilli. While I ate, I reviewed the same aspect I'd studied in the morning. Check. Double check.

In the evenings I tried different looks in front of the mirror – smoky kohl-rimmed eyes and red lips . . . false lashes, glossy lids and nude lips . . .

It was odd seeing myself with foundation-smoothed skin, blusher-enhanced cheek bones and sultry eyes, and a relief to wash it all off in the bath before dozing in the enormous bed. I didn't think about the fact that my parents had slept there. Everything to do with home was locked up in a corner of my brain – it was the only way I could stay strong.

Using Tor to stay anonymous, I Googled my name and Angel's. Dan was leaving messages for Angel everywhere we'd ever been. He was desperate to find me, and it wasn't because he was missing me . . .

I also kept an eye on the bookings page to make sure no one was planning a last-minute romantic weekend at my hide-away.

Every other day I went food shopping, using different stores and going at different times so I didn't ever see the same cashiers. I also varied my route and made sure no one saw me enter the property. I didn't chat to anyone, but wasn't in the slightest bit lonely. It's lonelier to be an outsider in a group than not in a group at all.

No one came to the house, not to shove a flyer through the door or check the meter.

Three days before my chosen date of 7th April, everything was ready.

The drone strike relied on sewing together thirteen separate elements – unlucky for some. I had the lines of code I needed to get into the US Military network and hack the drone, I had the fake video showing the drone crashing, the warning written, the code to take down the BBC home page, the route mapped from Germany to Norfolk and then from Norfolk down the coast to London, and the commands to fire. I had computers infected with bots, ready to bring London Transport's ticketing site crashing down. I'd repeatedly checked the timing plan. I'd thought of everything, thanks to Sayge. Our practice runs at planning attacks had been invaluable for thinking things through and paying attention to detail.

Two days before, I had diarrhoea. Classic case of nerves.

Doubt overwhelmed me.

I thought about going home, saw myself arrive at the front door, felt Mum's tears on my face as she wept with joy, heard myself say I was sorry, watched Dad kiss my forehead, let him take my bag . . .

Hijack day came.

23

Sunday 6th April. A little bit of tapping and the drone was under my control. More tapping and the live feed was replaced by a video of the UAV crashing. I put in the GPS co-ordinates and the drone knew where to go. That was all it took. Autopilot did the rest. I almost sympathised with the drone operators. It couldn't have felt less like I was wielding a weapon, or less like a war.

While the killing machine skimmed over the water towards British airspace, I made myself sleep for two hours. Being tired made for poor decision-making. I woke to find an independent site was already circulating a rumour that an American Predator had crashed in woodland somewhere in Germany. The fake feed had done its job!

I hadn't expected the news to leak so quickly, but it made no difference. For the foreseeable, the military would be looking for a wreck.

I checked the GPS co-ordinates of the drone every half-hour to make sure it was still keeping a low profile, looping over the trees of the Norfolk countryside. The whole point of stealth drones is that you can't detect them using radar. You can see them with your eyes, but the population of Norfolk is small and the sky is big. It was a calculated risk.

Online, word spread.

Was it a crash? Or a hoax? Or a cyber plot?

Wait and see!

Despite the temptation to get on with it, I stuck to my timing plan. The warning went up at noon, replacing the BBC News home page – courtesy of the sucker who thought Angel wanted to put up a plea for a cancer charity.

The US Predator Drone is in London. I haven't decided where to direct the missile strike yet. How does it feel, Londoners? Knowing you might be on a job or shopping and boom! Look to the sky at twelve noon Monday 7th April and think about all the people who are scared every day, like you are now, because of killer drones flying above them.

Pandemonium.

I watched the fallout from the squidgy sofa. In no time #April7 was trending on Twitter and I had yet another name – Dronejacker. Nice tag. Stories about drones dominated the media, just as I'd hoped. All sorts of theories appeared online, fun to read, most far from the truth. It was a *Guardian* journalist, a woman, who first suggested that Dronejacker was someone who had a personal problem with America's 'drone wars'.

The term 'collateral damage' started to appear.

Finally, a year and a half after my grandma's murder, I'd got the world talking about civilian deaths attributed to UAVs.

Life felt brilliant. There was I, only eighteen, single-handedly bringing London to its knees. The first ever collateral damage from a drone strike in Britain was hours away. Maybe the last ever collateral damage in Yemen was a step nearer too.

I was watching the late news when I got an unexpected message from the Secretary of State, delivered by the BBC no less.

'. . . *British Government does not negotiate with terrorists but in this instance the threat to the general public combined with the explicit nature of that threat has impelled the Secretary of State for Defence to ask for a dialogue. In this unprecedented move . . .*'

Dialogue was *exactly* what I'd wanted a lifetime ago, when no one would listen. The offer had come way too late.

I responded to the government using the BBC's Twitter feed, bang on midnight (using 149 characters) – another little trick I'd learnt from a pal.

The job goes ahead at noon. How does it feel, civilians, to be at the mercy of an unmanned

flying weapon? By the way, Dronejacker's good. I like it.

I made myself sleep again, although the adrenalin meant that it was fitful and full of crazy dreams. It was a mistake to have left such large chunks of time in the plan, but I hadn't imagined it would go so smoothly. I half-wished I'd flown the drone straight to London, but the chances were it would have been spotted before I had time to get everyone good and scared. Patience would pay off in the end.

My alarm went off at five in the morning. I made French toast and ate it at the breakfast bar with both the telly and my browser trained on the news.

There was a lot of speculation about what the target might be, ranging from Buckingham Palace to Arsenal's Emirates Stadium. No one was even close.

The icing on my Predator cake was to bring London Transport to a halt. At ten-thirty I activated the botnet that a whole community of hackers had helped me to build and launched a DDoS on London Transport's central servers. The ticketing system collapsed in front of my eyes.

Before I had a chance to congratulate myself, Twitter went ape – loads of hashtags referring to a statement on the BBC. I clicked.

The entire site had been taken down to send another message to me. This time it wasn't the government.

The person, known as Dronejacker, threatening to strike London at twelve noon with a missile fired from a stolen American drone calls himself Angel. He is a Black Hat. He recruited other hackers online by setting them challenges. I am one of them. I had no idea what he was planning. There are other people out there like me, I believe. We are innocent. Angel is in this house near South Creake, Fakenham, Norfolk.

There was an image from Google Maps together with the GPS co-ordinates of the house I was in.
What?

I am an elite hacker, but a White Hat. Please take me seriously. My name is Dan Langley and I live in St Albans Road, Bristol. I am 16. I tried to report him but no one took me seriously. Go and get him!

I had to read it twice, the second time out loud. Dan Langley knew where I was. And he'd told the world.
NO!

The shock was physical. I stood motionless for who knows how long, paralysed by panic.

Then my electric circuits zapped back into life. I grabbed my computer and the folder containing my new identity papers, fetched my wad of cash and my purse and ran out of the front door. I turned onto the road, thought again, and ran round the back and into the field next door. I followed the line of the hedge. It was a smart move because less than a minute later a fast car came from nowhere. I saw the roof as I was climbing a fence – it was a squad car. I ran through the next field and caught my breath for a minute by a gate that led out to a country lane.

All I could do was keep running, but more cars would arrive, with more police, and dogs. The road was too dangerous, but going across country would be too slow.

A Land Rover came along, ancient, I stepped out into the road with my thumb out. He carried on past . . . and then stopped.

Hallelujah!

I climbed up into the passenger seat to find a stereotypical ruddy-faced farmer in a waxed jacket.

'Thanks very much,' I said, using every ounce of self-control to keep my voice steady.

'If it hadn't been me, it'd have been no one,' he said gruffly.

'It is quiet round here,' I said, amazed that he couldn't hear my heart booming.

'That's the way I like it.'

Neither of us said another word.

I was in a super-tight spot, but thanks to Dan the police were looking for a boy, not a girl. I had a window of time to get somewhere busy and disappear.

A car raced up behind us. I looked round just as

the siren shattered the quiet. The farmer tutted, pulled over slightly, and let them go past. I concentrated on breathing. In and out. Nice and slow.

From nowhere a helicopter appeared, flying low, like my drone. I kept my stare straight ahead.

The farmer dropped me in Wells-next-the-Sea, without noticing I had no shoes on. Seriously, I had no shoes. And no chargers. And no phone.

My phone! My brain made the connection.

Way before I even knew he was going to be useful, when he'd offered to get me credit, I'd given Dan my number – or rather the number of the phone I used as Angel. He must have used the GSM network, or maybe triangulated my position from the power levels . . . He was brilliant and determined, I knew that. But I didn't expect him to use his skills to betray me. It was crazy. Surely I couldn't fail because I'd overlooked eleven digits?

Don't think about that now.

I bought a pair of Vans and a brown satchel big enough for my laptop, tried not to look shifty – which was virtually impossible – and caught a bus to Cromer. It was only a third full, but I sat next to an old lady. My brain couldn't work out whether I'd left any clues to my real identity, but worst-case scenario I had, so it was safer to appear to be with someone else.

We chatted about the floods, because she said it took her mind off the poor people in London and 'that wicked terrorist'.

Every single sentence was an effort. The adrenalin wasn't helping me this time. It was killing me.

Noon came and went. London, no doubt, sighed with relief. But I wasn't finished yet. As soon as I could get back online, the strike was going ahead.

In Cromer, I had my hair chopped off by a trainee – the only one with a free appointment. I ignored her attempts to talk –

'Going anywhere nice tonight?'

– so I could think.

I was gutted that Dan had betrayed me. Our friendship had felt real. I'd assumed, because he was the one who'd actually hacked the drone, he'd be the last person to confess. Surely he was risking a jail sentence . . .? I'd clearly underestimated his conscience. As I watched my long dark hair fall onto the grubby lino flooring, I wondered whether he'd have been quite so ready to turn me in if he'd known about the murders.

'Is that all right?' asked my stylist.

She was overweight and spotty, wearing black leggings and a tent of a top, but my hair looked great. A short bob with a fringe – it changed me completely.

'Lovely, thank you.'

Next door was an outdoor shop, so I bought a cagoule.

I couldn't decide whether to stick to public transport and risk the police being at the station or hitch and risk a lift from a nosy parker.

Which was safer? *No idea.*

I headed for the train station, but took a left because there were two police cars parked outside.

They were closing in on me.

I needed to act randomly so they couldn't double guess my next move.

Get a grip.

I walked along the road, only turning when a T-junction forced me to make a decision. I wondered whether to try to find a shed or a garage to hide in.

No.

My instinct told me I had to get as far away as possible.

Eventually I found myself on the outskirts of the town, where I dithered for a bit at a bus stop, pretending to read the timetable.

Every vehicle that came along made my heart race. My chances of escaping were getting slimmer by the second.

I glanced up at a black car travelling way too fast in my direction. Forced my stare back to the timetable. It braked. I waited for the doors to open ... saw myself in handcuffs with a hand forcing my head down as I got into the back ... but it carried on past the thirty-miles-per-hour sign.

I looked back to where the car had come from. There was another sign stuck in the hedge, a square hand-painted one.

As I got closer I could see it was an advert for one of those caravans that sells egg baps and coffee in polystyrene cups. I walked the mile there almost as fast as if I'd run.

There was a lorry, a blue Mercedes van and a battered BMW. I opted for the lorry.

'Student, are you?' the driver asked as we pulled out of the lay-by.

'Yes,' I said.

'I've had plenty a student willing to hop in there,' he said, indicating the bed behind the front seats.

Gross. That was the last thing I needed.

24

The lorry driver stopped to fill up with diesel somewhere near Cambridge, just past a bus stop. I hopped
out before he could offer me the use of his bedroll
again.

'Cheers!' I shouted, like the jolly student he believed
I was.

There was only one person waiting for a bus – a
bloke with a huge rucksack.

No!

The realisation almost made my cry out. I'd mentally
stripped the house in Norfolk of all my possessions,
certain that nothing could lead them to Samiya. But
had forgotten that Mum had written my name in
permanent marker inside the flap of my rucksack. How
long would it take to crosscheck my name with any
other records, like the missing persons register? No
time. I had to assume that not only did they know I
was a girl, but that I was a five-foot-four, eighteen-
year-old, mixed-race girl. A photo might already be
circulating . . .

I imagined my parents, holding hands on the doorstep, sobbing as they told reporters what a good girl

I was before the tragedy. I shut my eyes, hoping the picture might go away.

I got on the first bus that came along, as did my fellow traveller. We weaved through the English countryside for a few miles. Sticking to the idea that having no plan meant my behaviour couldn't be predicted, I got off at the bus station and got straight on another bus that was about to leave, purposely sitting next to an old dear again.

As I clocked up the miles, I began to feel more in control. Frightened, rather than petrified. But my concern for the drone grew. It was programmed to circle Norfolk until I sent it down the coast to London. What if someone spotted it before I could get back online? Or it ran out of fuel?

In Stevenage I dumped the cagoule and bought a dark-red hoodie, just in case anyone had noticed me earlier, and spent fifty-five valuable minutes in another hairdressers getting blonde streaks. I asked the stylist to rough-dry my hair to speed up the process. The person looking back at me in the mirror could have passed for Spanish, Italian . . . whatever I liked.

At the bus station I bought a newspaper and filled the crossword with nonsense while I waited for a coach to London. The busier the city, the more easily I'd be able to disappear.

'Excuse me,' said a voice.

I jumped up like I'd been electrocuted.

'I didn't mean to startle you,' said a fortyish man in

cords and a jumper. 'I wondered if you could keep an eye on my mum while I nip to the gents.'

I clocked the wheelchair and its white-haired passenger.

'No problem.'

Being jittery was a sure way of standing out. I forced my shoulder blades down my back and took a deep breath — the first in hours. I took a second.

'Going far?' I said to the old lady.

She moved her head a tiny bit and stared through me. Good. No need to make conversation.

The man came back thirty seconds later and wheeled her off. I made my way to the right coach bay and joined the queue.

The doors opened and people began to negotiate the steep steps. There was a woman with a party of five girls — one of whom had brown skin like me. I sat in the seat across the aisle from their noisy party and, as soon as the coach rolled out of the depot, set about making friends.

'Where are you all going?'

'To see *Matilda*,' said the mum.

People like to talk. I asked questions, and answered theirs with lies. Anyone watching would have assumed I was with the party, maybe an older sister . . .

We got to Victoria at six-thirty. I walked briskly to the Tube, picking up an *Evening Standard* on the way and tucking it under my arm. As far as I could tell, London was back to normal. My deadline had come and gone. The ticketing system was back up. Whatever chaos I'd caused earlier in the day with my DDoS had been repaired.

The Circle Line train came in two seconds – I sat down and started reading the paper. The front page was a photo of crowds of people pouring out of King's Cross, lots of them looking up, with the headline: *Dronejacker's Deadline Passes*. Inside there was much more, but nothing concrete. Crucially there was no mention of Samiya, and no photographs.

My knowledge of London was ropey. I needed somewhere I wouldn't be disturbed, that was open late. I opted for Marble Arch, so I switched to the Central Line at Notting Hill Gate.

When I reached street level I was pleased to see that the skies were clear – good flying weather. I bought a laptop charger from Maplin and went from there to a Costa on the Edgware Road that a random stranger said was open until ten. According to my rough calculations I was three miles from the target – far enough away to be safe.

I ordered a large hot chocolate – keen for a sugar rush – then sat by a wall socket and waited for the life to come back into my computer. I was worried that my VPN routing would already have been compromised, but thankfully my connection behaved as normal. Listening to the advice my many hacker friends had given me had paid off – knowing my name wasn't going to help anyone find the virtual me.

To get the Wi-Fi I had to sign in using an email address. They never validate it so it wasn't a problem – I pressed any old keys.

First job was to check the whereabouts of the drone. It was, as I'd hoped, still circling over the Norfolk/Suffolk border. I executed the code and took over manual control. Tick. I input the new GPS co-ordinates. The Predator automatically set a course down the coast. ETA 21:00. Target – Waterloo Station, aka the busiest train station in Europe.

I made myself eat half a panini while I scanned news reports from earlier in the day when the strike was imminent, and the post-noon hypotheses. Security forces said the threat level remained at critical. No one knew whether the missed deadline meant it was all over or just postponed. Except me. Everyone agreed that Dronejacker was also responsible for the DDoS. No one knew who I was, or, at least, the media didn't. Huge relief.

I took the folded-up photograph of *Jaddah*, Lamyah and me out of my purse.

Not long now.

When I left Costa, the drone was approaching Southend. Within an hour blood would be spilled. A single strike on London, to make people understand that using drones wasn't playing fair. The feeling was incredible. When news filtered through to Dad's village, there'd be a party – goat and khat.

I walked for ten minutes until I found another café. As soon as the deed was done, I'd kill time on a night bus.

'A peppermint tea, please, and the Wi-Fi password.'

'Coffeecoffee,' said the waiter.

I set up the VPN and ran the code. While I waited for the heads-up display to load, I wondered who would happen to be in the cross hairs . . . Lunchtime would have been busier, but even in the evening there would be casualties. They were not my concern – sacrifices had to be made for the greater good.

I was only one more command away from carnage . . .

The connection failed.

I tried again.

Nothing happened.

No matter how many times I tried, I couldn't establish the link.

My tea went cold.

The lines of code to transform my PC into an operations centre might as well have been a nursery rhyme. I was powerless. My expertise was in getting people to help me and splicing things together. No way could I reroute the connection.

Time ticked on. I persevered.

The café emptied. The waiter came and asked me if I wanted anything else. I had no choice but to leave. Try from somewhere else.

I shut my laptop just as a bloke poked his head out of the kitchens.

'They got the drone. Shot it down!' he yelled.

I put my laptop in the satchel. It was over.

25

I went from London to Swansea to Glasgow to Birmingham, too scared to check into a hotel. As the train approached Leeds, my final destination, I washed my armpits in the loos and, with a trembling hand, plastered my face in the cheap make-up I'd bought from a skanky chemist. I stank of three days' travelling and a lifetime's fear and disappointment. I was exhausted, and terrified of being recognised.

Samiya's life story, including the murders of Lamyah and *Jaddah*, was all over the papers, accompanied by one of two photos – a blurred one, with my eyes half closed and my hair long and straggly, and a school mug shot from Year 11. It was difficult to imagine anyone recognising me – the last-minute makeover had done its job – but that didn't stop me feeling wired.

There was no reason why anyone would trace me to Leeds – I had no links with the place – but Drone-jacker *was* the news. Who wouldn't be a bit jumpy?

All I had inside the rucksack I'd bought in London were a few clothes, a lot of cash, a new phone and my papers. I'd left my computer in a London wheelie bin, in case I'd accidentally left an online trail. I thought

I'd been careful, but somehow they'd found the drone and brought it down . . .

I waited for everyone else to get off the train and then walked through the carriages until I found what I was looking for – a discarded tourist map of Leeds. A quick look told me all I needed to know. Turn left, go through the town, carry on up Woodhouse Lane to Hyde Park – student territory. I didn't want to appear as though I didn't know where I was going.

I walked briskly along the platform.

The short-term plan was simple – to hide myself among the thousands of students. I kept repeating the name *Saffron* to make sure I reacted naturally when someone used my alias for the first time. That someone happened to be Mack.

'You a student?' he said.

I assumed the little boy in front of me was talking to someone else, but when I looked around I was the only person left on the platform.

'Yes,' I said.

'Are you getting a taxi?'

'No,' I said, wishing I'd ignored him.

I put my ticket into the slot and pushed the turnstile. He ducked underneath.

Great! I was trying to blend in while my sidekick was flouting the law. Luckily the guard was half asleep.

'Are you walking, then?'

'Yes,' I said. I'd get rid of him once we were out of the station.

'I'm Mack.'

Social niceties were so not top of my agenda, but I decided I might as well try out my new name.

'I'm Saffron,' I said. 'And I really don't want company.'

'Me neither,' he said, which bizarrely, given how frightened I felt, made me laugh.

I turned left out of the station, and he came too. There was a man in uniform bang in front of us. Instinctively I looked away, and as a result stumbled slightly. Mack noticed.

'It's only a traffic warden,' he said.

I needed to get a grip. If even a small boy could tell I was nervous, I'd be locked up in no time. I made a snap decision.

'Are you hungry?'

'Always,' he said.

'Know any good cafés?'

Mack grinned and led me down a back street to a burger bar. It was useful having him by my side. The world was looking for a solitary girl, whereas with him I was clearly one of a pair. I relaxed a little, the conversation slowing down my racing thoughts.

He asked for a cheeseburger, chips and a Fanta. I had the same. Your brain needs food and rest. I hadn't had enough of either.

'You smell,' he said.

'You don't have to sit so close,' I said. He'd squashed himself up next to me on a bench seat. I wondered if he was cold. I was wearing a hoodie, but all he had on was a grubby short-sleeved foot-ball shirt.

'I don't mind,' he said.

In between eating with his mouth open it became clear that he spent his time latching onto strangers, hoping for food, drink, money or all three.

'Where do you live?' I asked.

'Delph Lane.'

He'd clocked that I was a stranger, so I let him explain where it was. Turned out we were heading the same way. Suited me. I had a guide, in the shape of –

'How old are you, then?'

'Nine,' he said.

– a nine-year-old boy.

The walk up Woodhouse Lane was very fruitful. Two hours after meeting Mack, I had a place to stay.

I'd assumed I'd have to risk a hotel – at least for a few days – but Mack said there was a postcard adver-tising a room in the window of the Hyde Park Corner Post Office.

'Whereabouts?' I asked.

'Don't know,' he said.

'But you're the one who's telling me there's a room,' I said.

'The lady from the café said.'

It was like a word game. I persevered. It turned out that Mack couldn't read, but happened to be outside the Post Office when the lady from the café had quoted the ad, pointing out what an astronomical price it was. (He had several goes at 'astronomical'.)

I rang the number on the card and was invited straight round to the house, which was on Brudenell Road.

'You'll be the first viewing,' said the voice – young, male, southern.

Mack would have come with me, but as far I was concerned his job was done.

'Nice meeting you, Mack.'

'Same. See you around, Saffron.'

He disappeared off. I didn't give him another thought, because I had no idea he'd be part of my story.

26

I knew I'd take the room before I saw it. Being homeless meant being vulnerable. Like Maslow's Hierarchy
of Needs, shelter was my priority.

The landlord, Freddie, was a post-grad whose
generous parents had bought him a house. If he thought
it was odd that I wanted to move in right away, he
didn't say. Nor did he comment on the sparse luggage,
but I covered that anyway by saying, 'I've got some
stuff to pick up that I left with a friend.'

'Let me know if you want a hand,' he said.

I paid the deposit and the first month's rent in cash,
promising to set up a direct debit when I'd changed
banks. As far as Freddie was concerned I'd decided to
look for work in Leeds, because London was too
expensive.

'The other lodger's called Polly. She's a post-grad
like me. She's not here and I've got to go out. So . . .
make yourself at home, Saff.'

I waited in my room until I heard him leave and
then went to the bathroom, locked the door and ran
a bath. The water was blissfully hot. I had no toiletries
of my own, but there was some lemon zest shower

gel, so I helped myself. I felt disgusting. Dirty. A failure. And very, very alone. I sank down so deep that only my nose and eyes were above the waterline, like a hippo in a river. I needed to think. But the weariness was making it difficult. And the anger was clouding my judgement. All the way through the Dronejacker affair I'd been prepared for it to fail. So many things could have gone wrong. But they didn't. When I finally had control of the drone, I *knew* nothing could stop me. And yet, something did. Crushing. Seriously crushing. I needed to channel the feeling into something positive, or I'd drown in my own bitterness.

I heaved my overheated body out of the bath and realised I had no towel. There was a small, stripy, germ-ridden one slung on the radiator, which I reluctantly used.

I nipped back into my room in my filthy T-shirt and put on a pair of joggers and a hoodie, which were only slightly better.

I wanted to curl up on the mattress and sleep, but there was no bedding, so I made myself go in search of a decent-sized supermarket. I didn't want alarm bells ringing right away. Normal people had 'stuff'.

I filled a trolley with bedding, towels, toiletries, a Union Jack cushion, food, underwear, clothes and a burner phone – all paid for with yet more cash – and got a taxi back. Luckily Freddie was still out, because I was too tired to think of an explanation for the ridiculous number of orange plastic bags.

By eight-thirty on day one of Saffron Anderson's new life in Leeds, I had stir-fry in my belly, a made-up bed, three changes of clothes in the cupboard and the means to wash and clean my body *and* the bathroom. Not bad. My mood had lifted too. I hadn't chosen the easy path – that would have meant grieving for my grandma and moving on. I'd chosen to take a stand. My first attempt had failed. I decided right then that my second, whatever shape it might take, wouldn't.

I was slipping into sleep, thinking about the people who'd narrowly missed dying on the streets of London three days before, when I heard someone come in the front door. I was instantly wide-awake again, too recently in fight-or-flight mode to properly let go. I wondered who it was – Freddie or Polly? Wondered what they'd say if they knew their new lodger was Dronejacker.

PART 2

27

'You certainly seem to have packed a lot in,' said Liam, the manager, flicking back to the first page of my application form.

I nodded enthusiastically.

'I've always been a busy sort of person.' My voice was as clear and confident as when I'd said exactly the same to the bathroom mirror.

'And that's the sort of person we need,' he said, smiling.

The interview was almost over. Liam had gone through my carefully worded lies one by one and I'd answered him as though I'd lived through each of them. Practice makes perfect, as Mum used to say – except she was talking about eating spaghetti without slurping.

'One last question, Saffron. Where do you see yourself five years from now?'

Good question. And one I hadn't predicted.

'In your job, hopefully.'

'I can't argue with that,' he said, unable to suppress a grin.

He shuffled his papers together, then moved his chair back so he could stand up.

'Something about you . . . seems familiar . . .'

I dropped my head, took a second to get a grip.

'I've got that sort of face,' I said as I too stood up.

Liam walked back to the reception area with me. The next interviewee was already waiting, hunched over and picking his nails. No contest!

'We'll be in touch by the end of the week,' said Liam, shaking my hand.

'Thank you very much,' I replied, meeting his eyes – green flecked with brown.

You can tell a lot from someone's eyes. I'd ticked all his boxes, employment and otherwise. I glanced down at the new me – black trousers, black brogues, grey silky top – the whole look copied from *Grazia* magazine. Being Saffron Anderson was starting to feel good.

As I pushed open the door and felt the May breeze warm on my face, I wondered what he thought he saw in *my* eyes . . . Probably exactly what I let him. Keen. Organised. Personable. Bright. Pity he couldn't see any deeper, but then dark eyes are so much less transparent.

I walked home, all the way up Woodhouse Lane and through the park, convinced that I'd soon be the Customer Services Agent for a worldwide courier company. Poor Liam was going to end up regretting his decision. Shame – he seemed like a nice guy.

I knew I shouldn't be getting ahead of myself. The

job was only the first step, but it felt so good to be wrestling back control.

It had been a tricky few weeks, finding my feet in Leeds, but I was back on task.

28

No one was in. Good. I made a cup of tea and took it up to my room. Sharing a house wasn't ideal, but the fact that Freddie was so casual definitely was.

I had three hours until I was due at the pub for another evening of being chatted up by students and wiping up slops. I hated every second of it, but if Liam liked me as much as I thought he did, I wouldn't be doing it for much longer.

I fished my seventh-hand (according to the names inside the cover) chemistry book out from under the bed and got cracking. No way could I get talking to a proper chemist without appearing to have at least some idea of redox equilibria and condensation poly-merisation.

I was finished with technology and had gone back to basics. The internet, email, phones – they all left traces. Even if you were clever – zig-zagging the globe, leaping from server to server – there was no guarantee you were either invisible or anonymous. If I even tiptoed around the web I was risking everything. I'd single-handedly had security organisations on both sides of the Atlantic on the hop. People were looking for me. Looking hard. I needed to stay hidden, and that meant staying away from chatrooms and hackers, and browsing books not HTML.

I'd made two other decisions. I was going it alone – look where my faith in Sayge and Dan had got me – and this time it was going to be fast. It was twenty months since the killing. A countermove was long overdue.

Too soon, the key in the front door announced that Freddie was back.

'Saff!' he yelled up to me. 'You in?'

'No!' I yelled back, shoving the book away.

'Very funny.' He was already loping up the stairs for his daily dose of sarcasm. Not that I minded him. He was twenty-one – like Saffron! – and easy to get along with.

'How'd it go?' he asked.

'Good,' I said.

Freddie plonked himself on the end of my bed.

'Did they test out your parcel-wrapping?'

'Yes.' I leant forward slightly, earnest face. 'I had to wrap three odd-shaped objects against the clock, and there were penalties for using too much tape.'

'A straight answer would be nice, just for a change ...' He pushed his hair away from his face. The long locks were an act of rebellion. Along with the tattoo I'd spotted on his shoulder.

Mum gave me a fake tattoo once, a butterfly, chosen from a sheet that came in a party bag. Dad went ballistic, thinking it was permanent. When he realised you could wash it off, he let me put a rose on his shoulder. The memory made my heart stop. I couldn't begin to imagine how Mum and Dad were dealing with not just a lost daughter, but an evil one ...

I banished the thoughts – the past only got in the way. After all, I couldn't go back ...

'The interview was fine,' I said. 'They send stuff all over the world with stickers on. I can do that.'

'What's the money?'

I told him.

He wasn't impressed but managed to say, 'At least it's not minimum wage.'

It was annoying having to fake being strapped. I still had plenty of cash, but it would be far too complicated to invent a reason why a twenty-one-year-old would live in a shitty room in studentville if she was loaded. Better to be poor, reliant on wages from the pub, hoping for something better ...

'My folks are coming up to Leeds in a couple of weeks,' said Freddie. 'Why don't you come and pig out at their expense?'

I shook my head.

'Families aren't my thing.'

He glanced at the walls. Bare. Looked at the top of the chest of drawers. I could see the cogs whirring – he was looking for clues to my life. Fat chance. I could have printed some photos from the internet and framed them to keep him happy ... but the genius lay in keeping things as simple as possible. As far as Freddie was concerned, I didn't speak to my parents, ditto the rest of my family.

The less I invented, the smaller the chances of a hiccup. But I didn't want to appear isolated. So ever since I'd moved in, I'd been to the cinema at least twice a week coming back full of details about the film, or sometimes the pub or club I'd supposedly been in, the punters, the drunks on the bus, the imaginary friend I'd gone with . . .

Truths, like getting an income from the pub job, helped tether the fiction.

'Not all families are the same, Saff.'

His voice was kind. A warning bell went off in my head. Letting anyone get close would be a Mistake, capital M.

'They are to me, Freddie.' I was deliberately offhand. 'I'm going out anyway.'

'You can bring whoever you like back, you know,' said Freddie. 'It's *your* room.'

'Sure,' I said.

There was a silence that I didn't try to fill. He stood up, uncomfortable, which was what I wanted. But yet to deliver his parting shot.

'There's something not quite right about you, Saff.'

Get the hell out, I wanted to say, but I needed to keep things nice.

'I'm left field,' I said, a laugh in my voice.

If only he'd hide in his room like Polly. She was

doing some sort of research into eating disorders, but went to Birmingham every Thursday night to spend the weekend with her boyfriend.

Freddie was studying theoretical philosophy, but seemed more interested in studying me.

I shut the door behind him and, reluctantly, took my Union Jack cushion off the bed. I undid the zip and took out three press cuttings. One last look and then they had to go. Keeping them was an indulgence anyway, and indulgences weren't allowed. One was an analysis, published the Sunday after, of the 'frighteningly well-organised attack', heavily criticising the American security measures and praising the Brits for shooting down the drone. The second was a piece suggesting that I was in Syria with my jihadi friends. (Most reports assumed I'd left the country.) The third, my favourite, was a blistering attack on America's drone wars, and included a paragraph about Lamyah and *Jaddah*.

I got a lighter out of my rucksack, leant out of the window of my room and watched each piece burn. There was something symbolic about seeing the coverage reduced to ashes. Next time the ashes would be made of more than just typeface.

29

I got the call two days after the interview. It was gone eleven but I was still in bed, scribbling on my A4 writing pad. The shopping list of what I might need had turned into more of a mind map, with dashes connecting chemical compounds with their common names and less violent uses. Like potassium nitrate, aka saltpetre – handy for preserving meat, fertilising plants and as an oxidiser in explosives. Not that I was using that. I'd decided on the stuff they put in the cold packs you use on sore muscles – because you can buy them in Tesco.

I liked the unexpectedness of it – no one would imagine, after the complexity of the drone attack, that I would shun the internet in favour of chemistry, parcel tape and a worldwide courier operation. It wasn't anything like as audacious a plan, but all I was after was success. Bombs were a tried-and-tested method – and not that difficult to put together. Seriously, anyone who could follow a recipe for a Victoria sandwich had a bomb within their grasp. All I had to do was make one and decide where to send it.

'Is that Saffron Anderson?'

'Speaking,' I said.

'Hello, Saffron, it's Liam from SendEx.'

'Hi, Liam.'

He went through the main points of the offer, emphasising that if I was as good as he expected, the three-month contract would turn into a permanent position – not that I cared. Three months and I'd be gone. Job done. Staying anywhere for too long risked my past catching up with me.

Liam ended the call by saying that the paperwork would be in the post by end of play. I confirmed that I could start next Tuesday – Mondays were frantically busy, evidently, because there were no deliveries on Sunday.

Getting the job felt like a major achievement. Not only could I give up the bar work, but it meant I could start information gathering – see how difficult it was to send a bomb. There was bound to be screening at some point in the process. Until then, there wasn't much I could do, so I decided to take a walk in the park. I didn't reckon on company, but was quite glad of it.

'Saff!' It was Mack, truanting as usual. I saw him every few days. And most often fed him.

'What have I told you about that stuff?'

He was leaning against the toddler slide with a can of cider in his hand.

'There wasn't no milk,' he said, his grin showing his awful teeth.

'I got a job,' I said.

'I know,' said Mack. 'In the pub.'

'Not any more. From next Tuesday, I'm working for a company that sends things all over the world.'

'Can you send me?' said Mack. 'I want to go to Germany.'

'Why there?' I asked.

''Cos my dad's there.'

I didn't know he had a dad. His mum I knew all too well – she was barred from the pub, but still tried her luck when she was staggering and slurring but not yet in a coma. I'd refused to serve her a few times and she'd called me a selection of racist names. Nice.

'When did you last see him?'

'Never seen 'im.'

I didn't push it.

'Let's get a 99.'

Mack drained the can, tossed it onto the shiny green grass and walked with me towards the ice-cream van.

'Can I live with you?' he said.

'No,' I said. 'Why? Is something up?'

He shook his head.

'Can I see your flat?' he asked.

'I live in a house,' I said. 'And no, you can't. Someone'll call the police if I'm seen stealing a little boy like you.'

'They came to ours yesterday. Mum was yelling.'

'The police?'

He nodded.

'What for?'

Mack told me a variation of the now-familiar story. It seemed like every week his mum would go ape, accusing the downstairs neighbour of thieving, curtain-twitching, being black, being a benefits cheat . . .

This time, Mack's social workers had threatened to take him away.

'If they took me I could live with my sister,' he said, before pressing his finger on the picture of the Screwball. 'Can I have one of them?'

'Recognise any letters?' I asked.

'Scr,' he said, lying. It was pointless trying to teach him to read, but I did it anyway.

'I didn't know you had a sister.'

'You didn't ask me,' he said. Fair point.

We wandered to the swings and sat side by side. A few little kids were playing on the climbing frame, their mums gossiping on the bench. The *Big Issue* man came past and nodded at Mack, who gave him a thumbs-up.

'Have *you* got a sister?' he asked.

'No. I told you, I haven't got anyone.'

'You've got me.'

I pretended to slap my own forehead.

'So I have.'

He smiled. When he was happy, his filthy face, horrid teeth and grimy hair all disappeared, leaving just shining eyes. When he was sad, he looked like those kids on the posters for the NSPCC – only worse, because I knew him.

'Where's your mum, then?' he said.

'She died,' I said. Her face flashed in front of me – long brown wavy hair, lips always painted a rosy pink, a heavy gold necklace she never took off because Dad had bought it for her. I quickly pushed the picture back where it belonged.

'I wish my mum died,' he said.

The sun was starting to go down. I walked back with him towards Delph Lane. There were two police cars parked on Woodhouse Moor, the cops leaning on the bonnets, chatting.

'Get yourself fish 'n' chips,' I said, putting a tenner in Mack's sweaty little hand. 'I've got to go.'

'Thanks, Saff. I love you.'

He ran off. But his words stayed with me as I headed back to Brudenell Road. He wasn't part of the plan, but what harm could it do? After all, he was nine.

30

As I handed my completed forms over to the office manager on my first day at SendEx I had a second of doubt. What if I'd been duped? I'd paid a fortune to steal Saffron Anderson's identity with no guarantees. Cyber criminals don't give receipts. My pulse quickened, but I kept my gaze steady.

'Lovely name,' she said.

'Thank you.'

I wondered what had happened to the original Saffron. Dead, according to my supplier, but how? Car accident, cancer, stabbed by some mad man who'd escaped from an institution . . .?

As she ran through the basics like holiday entitlement and sickies, I studied her. She was tidy in the way that she spoke, dressed, wrote and filed her nails. Definitely not a risk-taker – her taste was too boring. She wasn't important, but it was good practice to notice things.

'I'll take you along to see Liam now.'

'Hello again, Saffron,' he said, from behind a seriously messy desk. It was a good sign. The less attention to detail he had, the better.

He took me on a tour, covering everything from the handheld PDAs the delivery drivers used to the pricing structures. I got it all first time, but let him drone on – he was clearly proud of their 'slick operation'.

Best not to appear too smart anyway.

In my hour's lunch break I went to a café and ordered a tandoori chicken flatbread. The telly was on in the corner – some news programme or other. I was watching the waitress, thinking about how most people did dull jobs, when a name caught my attention.

'. . . Dan Langley. Extradition laws were meant for terrorists, not kids exploring the internet from their bedrooms.'

The speaker – a scruffy bloke with a big, round face – was clearly Dan's lawyer.

'. . . The burden of proof, which underpins British law, barely exists in the powers our government has handed to the Americans, in what was a poorly-thought-through knee-jerk reaction to increasing threats of terror.'

It took more time than it should have for me to catch up with what was happening. Being back in the headlines was terrifying. I expected a photo of me to replace the lawyer any second. But didn't move . . .

'. . . I would ask the Home Secretary to quickly and decisively reject the extradition request and leave Dan Langley to continue with his GCSE exams.'

The presenter switched to the weather forecast.

The busybody on the next table switched to me.

'Chop his bloody head off, I would,' she said, looking at me. 'Little brat, helping that Dronejacker.'

I didn't respond. Just stood up and went to the ladies, cross that I'd drawn attention to myself by being so engrossed in the story. In the cubicle I let the breaking news sink in.

The Americans wanted Dan shipped over the Atlantic to be tried in their courts. What did that mean for me? It felt dangerous, but, thinking it through, I concluded that they were giving him flak because they couldn't find me. It wasn't ideal – what I needed was for the world to forget all about Dronejacker and move on – but it wasn't a disaster either. I wasn't an expert on extradition but I was pretty sure that Dan would be prohibited from talking about the case for the foreseeable, which would give the story time to fade.

As the shock receded, a grin found its way onto my face. Served him right. Without Dan Langley meddling, my plan would have succeeded. Without Dan Langley, I could have moved on. Instead, I had unfinished business.

I checked myself in the mirror. The light streaks and the heavy fringe made me a different person, helped by the ridiculous lashes. I reapplied my lip colour and left the café.

Relax, Saff.

The afternoon flew. I shadowed Elisa, who was one of the senior customer services agents. She processed parcels going everywhere from Wigan Pier to Phnom Penh in Cambodia. Seeing how simple it was to route stuff around the world, whether it was the size of a pin or an elephant, was reassuring. But there was more to it than putting an address on a stick of dynamite. I had to make sure my parcel arrived – which meant getting round the Dangerous Goods transport regulations. *And* exploded – which meant finding a way to get hold of some controlled substances. Not the sort that blew your mind, the sort that blew you up.

31

All too aware that I was in the top ten most wanted, I was reluctant to go online – but needs must. At lunchtime on Friday, I went to an internet café down by the station, opened a Hotmail account in Saffron's name and booked a place on Leeds University's open day at the end of June.

I hovered my fingers over the keys – so very tempted to Google Dan Langley and see how much trouble he was in. But I resisted. Browsing was safe enough, but I'd made the rule for my own protection. I needed to stay away from the forever footprints left tangled in the web. I logged out and bought a *Guardian* newspaper instead (and two more cold packs). There was an article arguing against Dan's extradition. It was very persuasive.

The afternoon dragged. Another weekend of deception lay ahead. I felt tired. Thought about going away somewhere – holing up in a hotel with a huge bed and a deep bath and being me.

Me. Interesting concept . . .

The first two weeks working at SendEx had been surprisingly nice. I could almost have forgotten why I was there, apart from the odd trip to buy a soldering iron from Maplins, and more than a few cold packs from Boots and Superdrug – all of which I'd deposited in my rented storage unit. The routine was oddly reassuring, comforting even. I chatted with Elisa and the others, went to Subway with them and swapped funny stories about the customers. Almost all the agents were young – although not as young as eighteen. The work was simple – just a question of being organised. Evidently the big boss had already congratulated Liam on recruiting me. Tempting though it was to start working out what obstacles I was going to have to negotiate to send a bomb, I'd resisted. Fitting in was the first step, and that had gone swimmingly. In fact, I was in danger of becoming Saffron Anderson inside as well as out . . .

Involuntarily, I shook my head, as though flinging that thought away.

'Got a flea in your ear?' said Elisa.

'Crick in my neck,' I said, ticking myself off for being weird.

Bang on five-thirty, I left work, catching the bus to Hyde Park because I couldn't be bothered to walk. I turned into my road, praying the house would be empty, to find Freddie standing by a white BMW X5. Parents. Alarm bells sounded in each compartment of my head. I was losing my touch. I'd forgotten his invitation to 'pig out', and had therefore also forgotten that there'd be visitors arriving. *I* didn't forget things. As I strolled towards the happy family I wondered whether the strain of being someone else 24/7 was too much. Undercover cops tended to crack up, didn't they? And they had training. I'd trained myself.

Doubt crept in. It was an alien feeling.

'Mum, Dad, this is Saff. My new lodger.'

'Pleased to meet you,' I said, holding out my hand.

The mum ignored it and gave me a half-hug – hands on my shoulders but body well away, cheeks almost touching, but not.

'What a beauty you are,' she said.

I felt my cheeks get hot. Not so much from the compliment as from the memory of my own mum. The sense that my hold on things was slipping grew stronger.

The dad was more reserved.

'Hello . . . *Saff.*'

'Short for Saffron,' I said. Before the conversation could continue I took control.

'I'm sorry but I've got a migraine.' I touched my forehead, made my eyes pained.

'Poor girl,' said Freddie's mum to my back.

Safe inside, I grabbed a glass of water and took it up to my room. I lay down on my bed, door locked, and played the movie of my life, starting with the summer in Yemen and ending with the train drawing into Leeds railway station two months ago. It calmed me. Focused me. Keeping up the pretence was going to be harder than I thought. I'd concentrated on the practicalities, ignoring the mental side of things. That was a bad call. On the internet it had been simple – face to face took the subterfuge to a different level. I needed to look after myself. Find time to relax.

There was a tap on the door.

'Are you all right?' It was Freddie, whispering – which was sensitive, for him. 'I'm off now.'

I didn't answer. He waited, then went back downstairs. The door slammed. The car started up outside my window.

All clear.

I sank into a deep sleep. My defences were down – that was the only explanation. Because for the first time since the drone strike, I had a dream about my grandma and Lamyah that didn't end up with them in a thousand pieces.

32

Freddie had left a note on the kitchen table that I didn't read until morning.

> *Hope head gets better.*
> *Freeloading at the hotel with Mum and Dad.*
> *See you Sunday.*
> *Freddie.*

I pressed my palms together and gave thanks to the God of People with Stolen Identities. Polly was away at her boyfriend's as usual, which meant I had a weekend to myself, just when I needed it.

I had a shower, pulled on leggings, flip-flops and a pink crop top and headed to the Spice Centre, opposite the mosque, to buy all the ingredients for my own 'pig out'. My basket was so heavy the handle was slicing through my hand. They gave me a box at the checkout – much easier.

Back home I made dough, just like my grandma had taught me. I put it in a hot pan and waited for the layers to separate. The mixture was ready – eggs, onions, coriander and chopped hot green chilli pepper. I spread it over the bottom, slapped the other layer on top and waited. The smell took me back. I let it. Not frightened any more of seeing the carnage. Sure I could conjure up happy times.

I pierced the dough with a fork. No ooze. Good job.

The kitchen was dark and depressing, so I took my breakfast outside and sat on the doorstep in the sunshine, with a mug of British tea.

I left the washing up and headed to the park, planning to walk into town to buy more cold packs and some other items, like electrical tape . . .

My storage unit on the Kirkstall Road already contained three pressure cookers of different sizes (one new, two from charity shops), a drill, a bucket, several brown cardboard boxes, a white lab coat and 118 cold packs – each of which contained liquid, which I didn't need, and little beads of ammonium nitrate, which I did need. Three hundred cold packs was the goal. It was slow-going, but buying too much of anything from one place was a mistake I wasn't about to make.

'Saff!' It was Mack, running across the park towards me.

'Hello, trouble,' I said. 'What are you up to?'

'Can we go to the café?' he asked.

I was going to refuse, but he looked a bit needy. Understatement!

He was starving. Said his mum hadn't come home.

I tried to work out since when, but Mack was hazy on the details.

'She went to get chips,' he said.

I bought him a full English and a cup of coffee in Chichini's, which the black-hair-with-a-white-stripe-down-the-middle waitress tried to give to me.

'It's for him,' I said.

She gave me a vile look.

'Isn't there anyone else?' I asked Mack. Then wished I hadn't.

Mack didn't seem to have any idea of family. Come to that, he only had a loose grip on time. And no sense of danger. After all, he'd made friends with me.

Not for the first time I thought about making an anonymous call to social services – but who knew whether that was the right thing to do?

'Saffron?'

I looked up to see Liam, in bright-yellow running kit.

'I thought that was you,' he said, adding a 'Hi' in Mack's direction.

"Ullo,' said Mack, chewing a lump of bacon with his mouth open.

'This is Liam,' I said. 'My boss.'

There was that tricky silence where one person expects to be invited to sit down while the other person waits for them to move on. I wasn't going to crack. But . . .

'Get a chair,' said Mack.

'Cheers,' said Liam.

Great!

'The usual?' shouted the waitress.

'Please,' said Liam, sitting down opposite Mack.

'Same every Saturday. Round the park, then fodder,' he explained.

I smiled.

'How was your week?'

'Good,' I said.

'She worked in the pub before,' said Mack. Chew. Chew.

I willed him to eat fast – which he always did anyway – so we could leave. Until then I needed to chat, to make sure Mack didn't.

'How long have you been at SendEx?' I asked.

'Four years,' said Liam. 'Started in your role, actually.'

'Good for you,' I said. Flattery always helps things along.

'Right place, right time. Someone left and . . .'

The small talk continued. Liam lived in a studio flat in Headingley. His parents lived on the other side of Leeds with his little brother. He didn't question me – it was all on my application. Saffron Anderson was a Londoner. End of.

Mack ran his finger round his plate, demolishing all traces of egg, bacon fat and brown sauce, then burped.

''Ave you got a car?' he said, his mouth at a loose end.

'No,' said Liam. Mack looked disappointed. Clearly a joyrider in the making.

'You smell bad,' said Mack, out of the blue.

'You're right, I do,' said Liam, looking down at his sweaty running top and laughing.

My traffic light flashed amber. I doubted whether Mack remembered saying exactly the same to me when I first met him at the train station – on the run from the police, MI5, Interpol and the FBI – but I didn't want to risk a blow-by-blow of how he'd found the homeless me a place to live.

'I don't feel very good,' said Mack.

'We'd better get you home, then,' I said, grabbing his skinny little arm and hoicking him up.

'Bye, Liam. See you on Monday.'

'Have a good weekend,' Liam called after us.

He probably thought it odd – the way we upped and left – but it was damage-limitation time.

'You don't like him,' said Mack as we walked towards his flat.

'Not much,' I agreed, but, actually, Liam was all right. Nice to grubby kids. Fit . . . I stopped myself. Thinking about sex led me straight to the bloody awful thing with Hugo – two years and it still made me cringe. I was usually a good judge of character, but not that time.

Halfway up Delph Lane, I said, 'Go and see if your mum's there.'

'What if she's not?' he said, still holding my hand, eyes like a baby rabbit's. His face was flushed – instinct made me reach out with my other hand. He was hot. The ill sort, not the weather sort.

'I'll wait here,' I said, smiling. 'Just in case.'

And then what?

Off he went, his slight body parcelled in once-orange shorts and an Arsenal shirt.

Mack knew stuff about me – harmless on the face of it, but if you knew what you were looking for . . . not quite so harmless. I'd arrived in Leeds three days after the failed drone attack. I was an apparently homeless girl of the right age carrying a single rucksack. Mack was the only witness.

I didn't wait.

33

I watched a documentary on telly about the White Widow – allegedly responsible for carnage in a Kenyan shopping centre and, like me, on the run. They interviewed her school friends and neighbours. It freaked me out. She came from Aylesbury – seventeen miles from Buckingham.

The idea that an investigative journalist might already be researching Angel's story whirred round in my head. Sleep took a while.

The night was never-ending. I was too hot, too cold, unhinged, locked up, locked out, frozen and, finally, burning. I took two paracetamol at about six in the morning, and two ibuprofen about ten minutes later, desperate to get my temperature down. Mum used to tell funny stories about my ravings when I had a fever – pinned down by sheets as heavy as lead, fish by my feet, a disembodied hand that kept slapping me.

I padded down to the kitchen in my pyjamas and, while the kettle boiled, took stock – sore throat, headache, achy everything else. So much for my weekend of peace.

I thought a short walk might help, but my legs told me otherwise.

Stress takes a toll on your body. Being constantly in fight-or-flight mode lowers your immune system, kills your heart and gives you diabetes.

I lay on the bed, flat on my back, breathing way too fast – couldn't get the memory of my frantic escape from Norfolk out of my head. That episode was over, but I still had to live every day in someone else's shoes, which meant being constantly vigilant, never relaxing, never off guard.

No wonder I'd succumbed so easily to what I was pretty sure was Mack's virus. Sleep was the only answer.

At some point I thought I heard Freddie. Or maybe Polly. My door opened and I thought about calling out, but when I looked again it was shut.

It was dark when I sat up with a start. I was suffocating, totally unable to swallow. I reached for the water glass, took a glug, but it stayed where it was – a pool, hovering in the way of my trachea, keeping the air out like a cork in a bottle. Panic. I staggered to the bathroom, heaved, threw up a tiny bit of bile. It hurt like hell.

Freddie's head appeared in the mirror.

'What's up?'

I made a rough choking noise. Held the side of the sink, worried I might faint. All I could do was concentrate on what little air I could force in.

Freddie disappeared.

The urge to swallow was overwhelming, but I couldn't make the spit come. I sank to the floor, vaguely aware of the fact that I hadn't cleaned it for a while. Concentrated on taking shallow little pants.

Two women in green came.

I tried to croak, pointed at my throat. They crouched down by my side in the tiny room, talking all the time but using words I couldn't decipher. One of them put a mask on me, and a bit later they managed to tie me into a stretcher chair. They carried me down the stairs and into the back of an ambulance. On what little oxygen was feeding my brain, I tried to work out what having no NHS number would mean to the staff. A glitch in the system? Or would it flag some kind of warning?

'They're taking you to Leeds General,' said Freddie's voice, loud and in my face. And then the doors were pushed shut, changing the light. I heard the engine start up and off we went.

I felt oddly detached, like I was watching myself in an episode of *Casualty*. The panic gave way to acceptance. I was ill. I didn't want to go to hospital, but I didn't want to die either. Not yet.

'Possibly strep,' someone said.

And then, 'Five minutes.'

The doors opened again and I was whisked into the hospital where a team was waiting to save my life. Noise and lights and voices, people moving around me. I let go of the worry. And let them get on with mending Saffron Anderson. I wouldn't die, because I still had a job to do.

Inshallah, as Dad would say.

Everything went black.

34

Several times I thought I was going to die. I didn't, clearly, but I lost a chunk of my life to intravenous antibiotics and a blood transfusion. Then, one afternoon, I woke up feeling better, clearer, more myself . . . but with no idea what day it was.

'She lives!' said a voice. It was Freddie, of course.

By the time I'd made my horribly dry mouth say 'Hi', he'd run off to get a nurse.

I think she was the boss – she talked like it anyway. I'd had an invasive strep A infection, it was Wednesday, I was lucky to have pulled through . . . blah-blah. I was nice and grateful, nodded a lot and then said I wanted to go home. The relief had given way to fear. I didn't want Saffron Anderson to have any more footprints than was necessary. Every new connection had the potential to trip me up.

'The doctor will do his rounds about five. He'll be able to give you an idea of when you might be discharged.'

'Thank you,' I rasped.

Freddie could see I wasn't up to our usual sarcastic exchange.

'I'll be back tonight,' he said.

I shook my head and made a don't-bother gesture.

I dozed while I waited for the doc. Mack's grubby little face kept appearing. What if he had an invasive strep A infection? Would his mum have called an ambulance? What if she'd gone AWOL again?

Liam!

I was seriously not on the ball. Hadn't given a thought to the fact that I'd missed three days of work.

I sat up with a weird dragging feeling, dizzy as hell. I took a few breaths and then tried to swing my legs over the side of the bed, but they got tangled in the sheets. I had a little wrestle with them, which exhausted me.

Damn!

I gathered enough strength to lever myself off the bed and then stood, wobbly like a two-legged foal. I still seemed to be attached to something . . .

'Get back in the bed, you,' said a blue-uniformed bloke.

'I need to make a call,' I said, already defeated by the idea. Whatever strep A was, it was still winning.

He lifted my legs back into the bed, like I was a granny. Took the details of my workplace and said he'd ring for me.

'Don't try to get up again,' he said. 'You've got a catheter.'

That made sense. Dan Langley's friend had a catheter after his run-in with a white van. We'd chatted about it online – he'd had to learn to pee again.

I dozed.

It was all very strange. In between the cotton-wool moments, I was sharp – worried about losing my job, worried about what I might have been saying – but I couldn't hold on to any of the thoughts long enough to make any contingency plans . . .

'Right, then.' The voice snapped me to attention. White coat. Brown skin, but not like mine. At a guess, some combination of African and north European.

The doctor repeated most of what the nurse had said. I had to stay on the antibiotics for a month. Might be discharged on Friday. I thought he was wrapping up, ready to charm the old dear in the next bed, but I was wrong. His team moved on, but he stayed.

'So, Saffron, you're a bit of a mystery. No next of kin. No visitors, I'm told, except a housemate who doesn't seem to know much about you. And no medical records, despite being . . .' He checked the clipboard '. . . twenty-one.'

I kept eye contact – looking away is a cue you're uncomfortable – but didn't reply.

'Can we contact a family member?' His eyebrows were raised, anticipating my negative answer.

'Estranged,' I said.

'Is there really no one? Not an aunt? A —'

'No,' I said.

He nodded, adopted a kindly voice.

'There are organisations that can help . . .'

Befriend a criminal mastermind today, said the sarcastic side of me. The other side was rattled.

'I'm fine,' I said. I didn't sound fine. 'I've got good friends.'

He didn't buy that – after all, where were they all? I willed my sluggish brain to come up with some reassurances to get rid of him. I didn't need a do-gooder interfering.

'Everything between us is confidential,' he said. 'No one will contact anyone without your say so.'

'You've got it all wrong,' I said. 'I'm fine.'

'Saffron!'

Perfect timing – it was Liam. I gave him a huge smile – genuine, for once. He introduced himself as a friend from work. I could have hugged him. His arrival did two things – got the doc off my back *and* made me seem less solitary. Good job.

'I feel really bad,' said Liam, perching on the bed – a bit too close to the tube carrying my wee. 'I thought perhaps you'd changed your mind about the job. People do that kind of thing. It never occurred to me you might be sick. Elisa was worried – I should have listened to her.'

'I'm really sorry,' I said. 'I was out of it.'

'Don't apologise,' he reached out and touched my hand. His skin felt nice.

'How are you? They said it could have been . . . much worse.'

'Shaky,' I said. I let the tears that were queuing up

have their way. It wouldn't hurt to show some vulner-ability, and anyway I couldn't stop them.

'You poor thing.'

He leant forward and put his arms round me, somehow avoiding the hospital paraphernalia. My body protested, but I made myself relax. It wasn't part of the plan, but it might be useful for us to be close. The more he liked me, the more he'd trust me.

I went one step further and, tentatively, hugged him back.

35

It was a week since I'd discharged myself from the hospital, clutching two boxes of pills and a copy of the note confirming that if I died it was my own fault. I'd been signed off work, which was a good job because although my throat felt fine, I was exhausted. In bed by nine and sometimes only waking a full twelve hours later. Apart from two short walks in Hyde Park – hoping to see Mack – I hadn't left the house. Freddie had been surprisingly kind, bringing me tomato soup and Ben & Jerry's. I tried not to remember being ill when I was little, with Mum making me hot-water bottles and stroking my hair.

There'd been no emotional appeals in the newspapers from my parents, asking me to give myself up, which was good and bad. Good, because seeing a tearful Mum and Dad whose lives I'd ruined would be pretty unbearable. Bad, because it meant we all knew there was no way back. The only home waiting for me was one with a lock on the outside.

The spell in Leeds General had made me feel vulnerable, physically and mentally. The longer I stuck around the more times my fake life would be tested. My answer was to sketch out the bones of a plan. Letting the side of me that had to stay hidden take control brought focus, and with it calm.

I didn't need to keep a tally to know that the numbers of civilians killed by drones had reached the thousands and didn't look like slowing down any time soon. Every time I read a report, my sense of responsibility grew. The anti-drone movement was increasingly vocal, but words weren't enough. Frederick Douglass tried words, so did the African National Congress. Sinn Féin did the talking, but it was the IRA's bombs that brought all sides to the table. Change had to be forced.

I worked all morning on my plans.

The first thing was to send a warning. I didn't want to use email . . . just in case some whizz somewhere could trace its source. I thought maybe half a dozen journalists could receive a letter by courier, explaining that an attack on US soil was imminent, signed Dronejacker. Just the mention of my nickname would guarantee a media frenzy. I wanted loads and loads of Americans to be frightened of what the skies might bring, just like the people in Yemen and Pakistan, just like the Londoners back in April.

I wanted the security services to be double-checking the whereabouts of all their drones, wondering whether I'd pulled off another hijack. There'd be no hint that the attack wasn't coming from the sky this time.

The bomb would be scheduled to arrive the day after the letters – everyday stuff for a courier company.

To get the names and addresses of the journalists I was going to have to go online again. When I had the worldwide web to help, I'd make the final decision about where to send the bomb. I had a few ideas . . .

I moved on to the composition of the bomb itself.

With a nice sharp pencil I drew lines and boxes, using the project management method I'd learnt when I was plotting with Sayge. The university open day at the end of June was a fixed point, and a lot depended on whether I found what I needed in their labs, but I made rough (by my standards) estimates and my best guess showed the critical path ending at the beginning of August. It was good to have a deadline to work to. I took the paper and burnt it.

Bored with being inside, and feeling a bit more energetic than I had for a while, I took Polly's student ID card (that she thought she'd lost) and decided to get acquainted with the university library.

I walked through Hyde Park, going via the play area, but Mack was nowhere to be seen. I considered wandering up to the flats where he lived, but my instinct told me to stay away. He wasn't my responsibility . . .

although the guilt of deserting him the day we met Liam in the café lingered.

Polly's card still worked, as expected. I knew she wouldn't have bothered reporting it yet – too lazy, too disorganised.

It was nice being in the library, pretending to be a student. I spent the first hour checking my understanding of both the chemistry of explosions and the physics and electronics of detonation, and then had a rifle through historical articles from the major news agencies.

Pressure-cooker bombs were reported to have been used in India, Algeria, Afghanistan, Nepal, Pakistan and, of course, Boston. I had no problem with copying, but I didn't want to copy the ones that had failed to explode or detonated too early. Mine had to be perfect, from the detonator – a mobile phone – to the explosive mix of chemicals and the packaging. There were published guidelines on what officials should look for in sorting offices, which included spelling mistakes on the label and wires poking out of the parcel – laughable. If that was the general level of expertise, I'd have no problems.

At about five I gave up on research and went home, pleased with the day's progress.

Freddie was listening to some unrecognisable music, playing something on his iPad *and* cooking. I missed the buzz of gaming, but Saffron pretended not to like that sort of thing.

'You look better,' he said.

'I think I am,' I said.

He flipped over his bacon.

'A few of us are going out – Brudenell Social Club. Want to come?'

I trotted out my normal excuse.

'Actually, I'm going to the —'

'Cinema,' he said.

I nodded and carried on past him, hoping to avoid any more questions because I hadn't bothered to see what was showing. Luckily his phone beeped, which distracted him. He started fumbling in his pockets in a bewildered fashion, and I went upstairs.

In my room, I heard the same message alert.

Bizarre. It wasn't Freddie's – it was mine.

I got my phone out of my bag and put in the four-digit passcode for the lock, mentally trawling through the few people that had my number – Freddie, Polly, work.

There was a voice message.

'I know you're off till Monday, but if you're feeling better I wondered if you wanted to go and see . . .'

It was Liam. Bosses really shouldn't hit on their employees. I hesitated, not sure if I wanted to take the risk. In hospital, getting close to him had seemed a good idea, but was it?

'Saff!' Freddie shouted up the stairs. 'What about meeting us at The Warehouse after for a boogie?'

That decided me. I needed Freddie off my case, and a film was a nice idea.

'I've got a kind of date,' I shouted back.

He whistled.

'Anyone I know?'

'Not if I can help it. Now leave me alone. I need to get ready.'

He went back to singing.

I arranged to meet Liam outside Sainsbury's, opposite the Hyde Park Picture House. He looked good, if you like blow-dries on boys.

'Hi,' I said.

He straight away kissed me on the cheek.

'You look much better.'

'I am,' I said. 'Thankfully.'

I bought chocolate from the supermarket while he queued to buy the tickets from the old-fashioned booth outside – it was more like a museum than a cinema.

Despite my reservations, we had a really nice evening. The film was *Ripley's Game* – he'd read the book.

'Didn't have you down as a literary type,' I said.

'Why's that? Because I look like a footballer?'

'Now you mention it.'

Afterwards we went to the Hyde Park pub and sat in the garden, where I bombarded him with questions so that he couldn't ask me any. Every answer made it harder for me not to like him.

'I feel like I've been interviewed,' he said as we walked out.

'That's only fair. You interviewed me first.'

It was the only time either of us had referred to work, which was good, because it seemed a bit creepy dating your boss.

I was thinking about how to stop him walking me all the way home when he said, 'As I've already broken the golden rule, might as well . . .'

Holy crap!

In an impossibly smooth move, he put his hand behind my head and pulled my face gently towards his. I could have avoided his lips in any number of ways, but I didn't have the willpower. Anarchists fancy people too.

36

I was at work bright and early on Monday morning, tiredness behind me, quite looking forward to seeing Liam. He hadn't been in contact since Friday – obviously playing it cool.

It took a while to get to my desk, as everyone wanted to know about my dramatic strep infection. When I made it, there was a bunch of pink daisy-looking things next to my computer. Didn't have Liam down as a flowers man.

'They're from me,' said Elisa.

'Thank you so much,' I said, genuinely touched.

'Lunch?' she said.

'OK.'

We left bang on twelve for an hour's shopping. I ate a sandwich while she tried on tiny dresses. Everything looked good thanks to her long legs.

I had to hand it to Liam – there was no hint that anything had gone on between us until five-thirty when . . .

'Fancy a drink after work?'

No, said my head.

'OK,' said my mouth.

'Twenty minutes, all right?'

'Sure.'

He suggested we go to the Belgrave Music Hall.

'Great,' I said. 'I've never been.' Although I knew where it was.

My first few days in Leeds I'd tramped the streets, getting my bearings, just in case I needed to make a quick getaway. The memory of being totally in control one minute, and running away from armed police the next, was still fresh. Maybe always would be . . . I shuddered.

It was strange. I was totally committed to unveiling the horrors of the drone wars, and yet there was a rebel bit of me that wanted, just for a while, to be Saffron Anderson for real. To have a boyfriend, and buy shoes I couldn't walk in. It was absurd. All my life – well, the last chunk of it anyway – had been about revenge. What was I thinking?

Shut up, Samiya, Saffron's having a fling, the answer came back.

'Ready?' said Liam, eighteen minutes later.

I nodded, pushing my fringe out of the way to give him the benefit of the mascara I'd applied in the loos.

We walked in step. It's funny how that happens without trying, even when you're different heights.

'I wanted to apologise,' he said. 'I didn't mean to . . . well, I did actually, but I don't want you to think that because you work for me —'

'I wanted you to kiss me,' I said, surprising myself. And him.

'You're extraordinary, you know. Unexpected. Bit scary, even.'

'You're right to be scared,' I said. 'I've got witch blood.'

'On your mum's side or your dad's?'

'Mum's, of course. Or it would be wizard blood.'

'Just checking you knew the difference,' he said.

It turned out he was driving later, so he had a Coke and I had a pear cider that we drank on the roof terrace. Nice.

'So what's the weirdest thing you've been asked to ship?' I asked.

'A hot tub,' he said. 'We arranged a pick-up and the driver got there to find it still full of water.'

'Seriously?'

'People can be *incredibly* stupid.'

'What else?'

'Nearly packaged up a kid once.'

I couldn't tell if it was true, but it was definitely funny. He said a kid had hidden in the drawer under a bed that was being shipped to India.

'Who was that little boy *you* were with?' he asked.

It was so odd not seeing Mack – normally I couldn't get away from him.

'In the café,' prompted Liam.

'Just someone I met,' I said. 'He's a sort of stray I feed occasionally.'

'He looked a bit uncared for. Poor kid.'

The caring side of me, which was so well hidden even I could hardly find it, wanted to grab Liam's hand and go and face Mack's drunken excuse for a mother. Luckily, I was good at suppressing kind thoughts.

I changed the subject back to the SendEx operation, hoping to get him talking about any X-rays or scans that might interfere with the grand plan.

'What aren't you allowed to send?'

'Kids, like I said.'

'No, really.'

'OK, starting with A. Aerosols not for personal use, asbestos, ammunition, batteries, clinical waste, controlled drugs . . .'

'Surely people are always sending batteries. Every good toy needs a battery.'

'If the battery's attached to a "device", then you can send it, but there are restrictions. This is dull, Saffron. And *you* are far too conscientious.'

We moved on to how much he liked bears and how much I liked cheese on toast (with paprika).

'I'm picking up my brother from Cubs or I'd have loved to take you for one, or maybe even two, pieces of cheese on toast . . .'

'Another time,' I said.

'Tomorrow?'

Brakes! shouted the sensible girl inside.

'Thursday?' I said.

'You're on.' He got out his phone to put me in his

calendar and, like all iPhone users, couldn't resist a quick check of his mobile apps.

'Guess what's trending on Twitter,' he said.

'No idea.'

'Hashtag Save Dan Langley.'

'Is he the Dronejacker kid?' Less-than-interested voice.

'Yes, he's the one they want to extradite. Look there's a video.'

Liam and I watching Dan talk about Dronejacker? Not a good idea.

'I thought you had to go,' I said.

'I've got a few minutes.'

We spent them kissing instead – an all-round better solution.

I couldn't imagine how Dan had whipped up enough support to be trending. My certainty that the past couldn't catch up with me faltered. I needed to know what *exactly* was going on, and that meant breaking the rules again and going online.

37

I left Liam to catch his bus and went straight to the university's Edward Boyle Library, using Polly's student ID to get in. I worked out her username by shoulder surfing – it was a combination of the department, the year of entry and her initials. Her password was equally straightforward.

In no time, I was up to speed. Dan Langley had been busy unpicking my plot in an attempt to clear his name. Somehow he'd made contact with Annacando, the American girl who'd given me tons of bots. She, unbelievably, had made a YouTube video confessing her part and declaring in pseudo-legal words that neither she nor Dan knew what I was up to. All true. I watched it twice with the volume right down. At one point she stared at the camera and said, 'She is the only criminal,' meaning me. It was quite powerful, helped by her accent and the fact that she was only eleven. The video had only been up for two days and she'd had over 200,000 hits!

More incredible still, her actions had given another of my recruits a guilty conscience – the guy who'd made the simulation of a drone crashing into a forest had fessed up too.

The revelations had snowballed into a whole campaign to try to save Dan from being extradited. Interesting, given that whichever way you looked at it, he *was* guilty of hacking the US Military and stealing a Predator drone.

All the coverage was focused on the hearing, set for a week's time, not the original crime – which was a huge relief. I was only mentioned in passing, accompanied by the usual unrecognisable photo.

I decided to take a calculated risk and watch the kind of YouTube video that *does* put you on GCHQ's radar – a tutorial on how to make a remote detonator. I could still remember the basic method from when I was trying to impress Sayge but wanted to see it once more. The university IP address was firmly planted in Leeds, but there were thousands of students who might want to remotely detonate fireworks . . . The chances of one dodgy search being picked up were tiny.

I paid close attention, memorising each step, and then reluctantly logged off. I wanted to stay and research possible targets for the bomb, but the library closed at eight and anyway, it felt like I was pushing my luck. Another day . . .

The cider had given me the munchies, so I took a diversion via the chip shop.

I ambled through Hyde Park, eating, and thinking, not for the first time, about what I'd be doing now if Dan hadn't ruined everything.

'What you staring at, bitch?' The words snapped me out of my daydream.

A familiar face appeared out of the shadows – Mack's mum, Maggie.

'Nothing,' I said, speeding up to get away from her.

'It's your fault,' she shouted, grabbing my shoulder and digging her nails in. I batted her away. She stumbled.

My instinct was to leg it, but . . .

'What's my fault?'

'Why don't you go back to where you come from?'

Did she know who I was, or was she just off her head?

'Toffee-nosed cow from the pub – I know who you are.'

There was my answer.

'I haven't seen Mack lately,' I said, keeping my distance. I pictured Mack's hot little face the last time I saw him.

'Not bloody likely to,' she said, and lunged at me. I should have been fast enough to step out of the way, but she fell like a boulder, all twenty-plus stone of her. I landed on the bony bit of my bum with one of her tree-trunk legs on top of me.

'Get off me!'

In the few seconds it took to untangle myself from her vile, sweaty body and escape her sickly-sweet breath, two blokes in uniform appeared. I should have known better than to walk through the park at dusk – it was full of troublemakers and cops.

'Up you get, Maggie,' said the one with a moustache, clearly familiar with Mack's mum.

'And you are?' he said to me.

I looked away.

Snap decisions – you have to be able to make snap decisions. I didn't want to give my name. I couldn't give a false name, because, drunk though she was, Maggie might know my name from the pub and tell them I was lying. So I ran. Wrong word for it – I sprinted. It was suspicious behaviour, but they probably wouldn't recognise me again, and if they asked Mack's mum who I was and she remembered where I used to work, the bar manager would deny knowing me because we had a cash-in-hand arrangement. It was the best move, under the circumstances.

The cop called after me. Some reassurance that I wasn't in trouble. Little did he know.

Instead of going straight through the park I took a detour, in case they were waiting on the other side. I didn't want to be on their radar. The chance of a bored copper delving into the history of Saffron Anderson was remote, but not one I wanted to take.

Only when I was safe in my room did I let myself consider what Mack's mum meant when she said I wouldn't be seeing Mack anytime soon. Surely he wasn't . . .

Damn that boy! I should never have been kind to him.

38

On the way into work the next day I gave myself a talking to. Saffron Anderson had a record on the NHS, someone using a Leeds IP address had shown far too much interest in the Dronejacker affair before searching for how to build a remote detonator and my face had been eyeballed by the police. It was only a matter of time before I had a brush with authority that led to some seriously awkward questions. I needed to knuckle down.

In the first lull I had, I checked the restrictions on sending batteries internationally – because a mobile phone without a battery wasn't going to ignite anything – and went through the security screening procedures. My conclusions were that I needed to send the parcel from a business account, and there needed to be a legitimate reason for the lithium-ion battery inside.

When Elisa brought me my mid-morning coffee she asked if I wanted to go to Harvey Nicks at lunch.

'Not today, thanks.'

'There's a sale.'

'Out of my range,' I said.

Instead I bought a cold pack in every stockist I

sauntered past, and put them in the lockable cabinet attached to my desk when I got back. It was a tedious business. I considered placing a bulk order with the manufacturer, even looked up the number and wrote a little script to use on the phone. I thought I could ask for it to be sent by SendEx to the physio place round the corner, and intercept the delivery. Luckily, I came to my senses before I did anything. The security agencies issued warnings about products containing ammonium nitrate, which included cold packs. A big new order might attract attention. Better to stick to the strategy. Hare and the tortoise and all that.

I came out of work to find that the clouds had disappeared and the sun was hot, so I walked home. There were loads of kids in the park, shouting and laughing, kicking balls and cycling – and one girl standing completely still.

She was flying a quadcopter, like a helicopter but with four rotating blades. I watched her manoeuvre it. My brain automatically added missiles.

She saw me looking.

'That looks fun,' I said, walking past with something new to think about.

I made chilli con carne for Freddie and Polly, because we'd agreed to eat together once a week on a Tuesday, and it was my turn first. It was delicious because I used my secret ingredient, chorizo.

'I vote Saff does all the cooking,' proposed Freddie, 'because I can't match this. Deal, or no deal?'

Polly was too busy adding a photo of her dinner to her Snapchat Story to answer, so I said, 'Deal,' which surprised Freddie.

Until I said, 'And you, Freddie, can do the bins and the recycling *every* week. And Polly, you can clear up. I'd be happy with that.'

'Deal,' they both said.

I left them to it.

I got myself comfy in bed, flicked open my A4 pad and drew six quadcopters. What if, instead of a warning letter, I sent each journalist a parcel containing a letter *and* a quadcopter? A quadcopter was a toy drone – the symbolism was nice. That was what PR was all about – using gimmicks to get publicity.

I drifted off with a little made-up video playing in my head. One of my parcels was in the middle of a huge room, surrounded by armed guards pointing their guns at it, when out flew a mini-drone. Neat.

39

Wednesday, Elisa was off sick.

'Hangover,' said the receptionist.

So it was frantically busy.

Just after eleven Liam came to see how I was coping.

'Fine,' I said. 'I've done the same-day deliveries, sent the pick-up schedules and I'm going on the phones at two.'

Liam's boss believed in rotating the tasks so we could all do everything. It suited me. I now knew how to prepare quotes, process orders, sort by weight and destination, take payment, track and solve customer queries. I also knew Liam had been in the monthly results meeting, because I'd given myself access to his digital calendar.

'Do you mind only taking half an hour for lunch?' he asked.

'No, that's fine.'

'Great. Thanks.' He winked.

In the end, lunch took a back seat.

'Saffron, can you go on the phones at twelve. Everyone's chosen today to ring up for a chat!' said the team leader.

'Sure.'

I spent the next hour dealing with idiots asking stupid things like, 'I'd like a pick-up at my office, but I'm not sure when it will be ready. Can your driver call me when he's passing?'

And, 'I sent a parcel last October, or maybe it was November, and my daughter says she never got it.'

But then I took a call from a theatrical make-up company in Beeston and learnt a few more things.

'I hardly dare say it, but we're really busy, and I'm pretty sure spending half my day in the queue at the Post Office isn't the best use of my time.'

He wanted to arrange a daily pick-up. Usually I'd have passed it to Elisa . . .

'Can I put you on hold for a second while I find someone to help you?'

'Do you mean a second, or half an hour?' he asked.

'I mean about twenty seconds.'

'Right you are.'

The team leader was only too happy for me to set up the account with her sitting next to me, showing me how. It was the usual stuff – name, address, nature of the business, bank account details, blah-blah . . .

'Would the packages contain any of the following restricted items?'

I read the list.

'We send nail varnish . . .'

I explained the volume restriction and he agreed to abide by the rules, and that was that. Subject to checks, he was set up on our system, and I was one layer deeper into the SendEx systems.

After work I went to Gadget Man in the Trinity shopping centre to see what quadcopters they had in stock. The sales assistant, who looked about ten, let me have a go with a 400-quid Phantom GPS Drone. He was very attentive — obviously paid on commission.

'Is it for your boyfriend?' he asked, entirely sexist, like the silly name of the shop.

'No, it's for me,' I said.

I flew it round the shop, narrowly missed crashing it into a glass cabinet and then said, 'I'm definitely having one —'

His eyes widened.

'— but not this one.'

I didn't want to spend thousands on toys that would most likely end up as evidence. I chose one for ninety pounds. *Probably only cost a tenner to make*, I thought. And that led to more thoughts. Why not send the bomb to a *manufacturer* of military drones? The very place the evil machines were created. The place that profited from their growing popularity. I parked the idea until I could find out more.

'I finish at six,' said the sales guy. 'So if you wanted me to charge it up and then give you a bit of a lesson —'

'I'm good, thanks.'

The quadcopter was half a metre squared. The box

was the size of a planet. I went shopping for some other bits and bobs I needed, including a cheap phone, and then caught a bus to the storage facility, laden with bags.

The whole place was deserted as usual. Alan, the manager, was there between eight and six, supposedly, so I always went after that. Not that there was anything incriminating for him to see.

I let myself in, took off my jacket, spent a few minutes tidying, then put everything I needed in the space I'd made on the floor. Time to make a detonator.

Sitting cross-legged, I took the soldering iron out of the box and read the instructions before filling it with lighter gas.

Fifty minutes later I'd taken apart the new phone, found the vibrator, cut a hole, done a bit of soldering, put it back together, added a relay and a battery, and was ready to try it out. I used crocodile clips to join the wires that were poking out to a circuit board with a bulb. If it lit up, I was in business.

I stood up, brushed the dust off my trousers and rolled my shoulders a couple of times – I smelt bad! It was the concentration.

My phone was in my jacket pocket. I got it out, tapped the number in and pressed Call, eyes trained on my contraption. The new phone did nothing. The bulb remained unlit.

Somewhere along the line, I'd messed up.

It was gone seven and I was tired and hungry – not

the best time to start again. *But I could just check each part*, I thought.

Using my finger as though I was doing guided reading in the infants, I followed the circuit round. It all looked good, but clearly wasn't.

I got my own phone out again and saw the symbol for signal leap from zero to two bars.

Silly girl. Can't make a call without coverage!

I tried again. The default ringtone gave me a bit of a shock, sounding far too loud in the deserted building, but the bulb still didn't light up.

Flummoxed.

I closed my eyes and tried to recall the YouTube video. It was really badly done, white text on a black screen, rubbish photos and no audio.

That was it!

I switched the phone to vibrate mode, keyed in the number – third time lucky. The bulb shone brightly for me.

Job done.

40

The next morning I ate my muesli deep in thought.

Sending quadcopters was one way of making my point – guaranteed, I'd get more coverage of the drone wars by using toy versions. But how much more dramatic would it be if I decorated each quadcopter with the story of an innocent victim? A glued-on photo, a name scrawled in permanent ink and a date would point the journalists in whatever direction I chose to send them.

Quadcopters, or similar, were also the answer to the battery issue. All I had to do was scan SendEx's list of business accounts to find one that regularly sent items with batteries and slide my parcels, and the appropriate paperwork, in among theirs. It felt right.

Polly walked into the kitchen with her phone pressed to her ear. It was unusual to see her up before I left . . .

Damn!

I ran to the bus stop, twenty minutes later than usual, and arrived at work at ten past nine to find Elisa back at her desk. Good on two counts. Nice company for me, and less work to do – which meant more time to concentrate on my other job.

'Are you better?' I asked.

'Yes,' said a deep, gritty voice.

'You don't sound it,' I said, half-laughing.

'It doesn't hurt,' she growled.

'The receptionist said you were hungover.'

'I wish.'

I raced through my admin and was about to get the coffees when the team leader came over with a wad of papers.

'Saffron, these are the documents we need to attach to the business account you opened yesterday to make it active. Do you want to do it?'

'Yes, of course.'

'Elisa, have you got time to show her?'

'Only if you promise not to give her my job,' replied Elisa, before looking across at me and saying, 'Teacher's pet,' still in a gravelly voice, utterly at odds with her pretty face.

More laughing.

Elisa showed me the ropes, and as she had a few more new customers waiting to be processed she gave me those too.

'I'll get the coffees, you do the work, keener,' she said.

'Yes, boss,' I said, in what I hoped was a Southern drawl. Banter was good.

Like all the other jobs at SendEx, it was simply a case of working through the screens, putting the right information in the right place. I activated the theatrical make-up man's account, drank my coffee and had the obligatory ten-minute chat with Elisa, and then did the three others that she'd given me. One of them was shipping hazardous materials that needed special labels, like my parcels would – handy to know how to prepare the documentation for that.

To check I'd done it all correctly, I went to the list of business accounts. The new ones hadn't shown up, so I refreshed the page.

'Elisa, I've done what you said, but the accounts still aren't live.'

'They need to be signed off by a senior manager,' she said, getting up and coming round to my desk.

She logged me out and logged in as Liam, typing in his password as quickly as she did her own. I memorised the pattern her fingers made – easier than trying to get the actual password in one go. The new accounts had red boxes by them that turned green when she clicked them.

'All done.'

'Don't you get in trouble for doing that?' I asked.

'Liam takes too long to get round to things. He knows I do it.'

'So should I ask him or you?'

'Depends if you want it done today or in a week.' Raised eyebrows, plucked to form a perfect arch.

She went back to her desk. I practised mimicking the way she'd typed Liam's password and then tried it out for real. Worked a treat.

Back on my login, I called up the list of business accounts. Halfway down I'd seen a name I recognised. I accessed their account.

Gadget Man had been a customer since 2010, had forty-five stores as well as a website and was in our top twenty in terms of volume. They were invoiced on the first of each month. Last month's showed that we'd shipped 132 parcels for them, of varying weights and dimensions – over half contained restricted items. My six would never be noticed. It was perfect.

Liam, looking particularly nice in a black-and-grey stripy shirt, came over when I got back from lunch.

'Thanks for covering for Elisa yesterday.'

'It's fine, I like being busy,' I said.

'Still all right for tonight?' he asked in a slightly quieter voice.

I nodded. Despite the voice in my head telling me to be careful, I was looking forward to dinner. Everything was going so well, I deserved some R&R.

Back at Brudenell Road, Freddie was in the kitchen, singing.

'Hey, Saff! I'm making an omelette, want some?'

I peered at the frying pan.

'Going out for something a bit more swanky, sorry.'

'With the guy from work?'

'Maybe . . .'

'Shouldn't mix business with pleasure,' he said.

'You really should, Freddie. It makes the day go so much faster.'

'You're trouble, Saff Anderson!'

'Not so much,' I said.

'Nearly forgot,' he said, 'you *are* in trouble. A policeman came round yesterday – about this time. Something about you running away after a "set-to" with the local drunk.'

'It was nothing,' I said. 'And I didn't run away, I just didn't stick around.'

I planted my bum on the edge of the kitchen table. It was easier to look calm sitting down. Inside I was jelly.

'How did he know where I lived?'

'Didn't ask. But he seemed to know you used to work in the pub. Maybe you served him . . .'

I knew I hadn't. Mack's mum must have told him.

'Anyway, I told him you were at work and he left a card,' said Freddie. He unclipped it from the fridge and read the name: 'Sergeant Collins.'

'Bit of an overeager copper,' I said.

'He had an overeager moustache,' said Freddie, flipping his omelette.

As I got dressed in skinny black jeans and a silky red top, I cursed my bad luck. It was like someone was testing me, showing me how much easier it would be to give up, marry Liam and have cute kids with green-flecked eyes. But that wasn't an option. After all, Lamyah would never get to have kids.

It was the open day on Saturday. I needed to finalise the composition of the explosive, based on what I found in the labs, then it was time to pin down exactly where my parcels were going. Six journalists would open a box and get a surprise.

The seventh . . .

41

Liam asked me to go back to his flat, but I wasn't ready.

'Dinner was great,' I said, 'but you know . . . work tomorrow.'

He didn't put any pressure on – not his style. I got off at the corner of Hyde Park, leaving him on the bus.

Walking back to the house, a full-blown argument was going on in my head. The two opposing positions were:

As long as it doesn't get in the way, why not enjoy yourself?

versus

Why jeopardise what really matters by getting close to someone?

I fell asleep in a stand-off with myself.

And woke on Friday to find a note from Freddie.

Gone to the Lake District – yomping!
Back tomorrow.

Polly had, as usual, gone to Birmingham for the weekend. I went into Freddie's room for a nosy, hoping that 'yomping' didn't require technology. The room was a pit — duvet half on the carpet, mould floating on what was once coffee, boxers . . .

But there on the desk was his laptop.

Thank you, Freddie.

It was too good an opportunity to miss. I called work and left a message, saying I had a sore throat and wouldn't be in. Texted Liam saying the same. It was good timing, because I was off to the uni open day in the morning — being ill was the perfect excuse for keeping Liam at arm's length for a couple of days.

A text pinged back:

Shall I come and visit after work?

might be sleeping, feel really rough x

Armed with a small, strong coffee, I settled down in front of Freddie's computer, which he hadn't bothered to password-protect.

First job was to choose a target for the bomb itself. I downloaded a Tor browser to scramble the source IP address and got Googling.

Typing 'military UAV manufacturers' into the search box was immediately fruitful. It wasn't as niche a market as I'd expected — there were quite a few, but one stood out. A company well known for flying holiday-makers across the Atlantic — that had obviously diversified. I used an SQL injection exploit to get inside the firewall and rummage, looking for the home address of the chief executive – I didn't want the bomb exploding in a deserted post room. I found it, and then checked the rest of his HR records. He had a family, a week's holiday booked for August and a medical overdue. There was a photo – a man with grey hair and a tanned face, wearing a crisp navy-and-white checked shirt.

Don't think about the individual, think about society.

I replaced the image with the Frederick Douglass quote that had stayed with me:

. . . they want the ocean without the awful roar, they want rain without thunder and lightning . . .

I moved on to the journalists.

The six largest cities in the US, according to Wikipedia, were New York, Los Angeles, Chicago, Houston, Philadelphia, Phoenix. I jotted down the names of journalists working in each of them, and then scanned examples of their work. I whittled the list down, based on the size of publication they worked for and what I could deduce about their politics. The last step was to hack into their Facebook accounts and LinkedIn profiles to really get to know them.

I made a second coffee, reviewed the information and made my choices. I copied the names and addresses onto the sheet of A4 below the chief exec's details.

The last job was to pick five innocent victims of drone strikes to focus the journalists' attention. I chose carefully, looking for the most heart-rending cases. The sixth victim was, of course, my Lamyah. I didn't think Jaddah would like having her photo stuck on a drone, given that she'd never left the village, but her story was intertwined with Lamyah's.

Their faces came shooting out of Freddie's printer, but I didn't look at them.

By three in the afternoon, I was finished — browsing history erased, Tor uninstalled, laptop back where I found it.

I'd been sitting for too long, so I went to find food and fresh air.

But instead found Mack.

42

Mack was sitting on a bench. I was so convinced he'd died of strep A, it took me a moment to speak.

'Where have you been, Mack?'

'With a foster carer.'

That explained the clean jeans and T-shirt.

'You look good,' I said.

'Can we get something to eat?'

'Sure can. I think we deserve a cake.'

We went to Chichini's and were served by the black-hair-with-a-white-stripe-down-the-middle wait-ress as usual.

'Was it nice at the foster place?' I asked.

'They had toilet wipes,' he said.

'Is that all you've got to say about it?'

Mack took a bite of chocolate brownie.

'And made me do Play-Doh.'

'That sounds nice.'

'Play-Doh's for kids,' he said.

'And you are?'

'Mack,' he said, as though I was stupid.

'So you're back with your mum, now?'

'Can I take one home for her?'

'A brownie?'

He nodded. Things had obviously improved.

While Mack finished his coffee I bought two take-away brownies, more than happy to invest in his relationship with his mum.

'Thanks,' he said, taking the paper bag. 'I missed you, Saff.'

I'd missed him too, but wasn't about to say so.

'Do you remember when we first met?' I asked.

'At the station.'

'I said "when", not "where".'

'Christmas, wasn't it?' He clearly didn't have a clue, which was good, because it meant I didn't need to worry about him landing me in it.

43

The Saturday of the open day was rainy, so I wore a silly spotted Cath Kidston cagoule. I'd got quite good at buying things that Saffron liked, but Samiya wouldn't have been seen dead in. Saffron had what *Grazia* would call 'a capsule wardrobe' for work, a lot of red and pink for play and an over-flowing make-up bag. I despised the articles in the magazines – obsessed with celebrity – but Saffron Anderson quite liked them. She bought it every week – part of the disguise, she told herself. A fashion-conscious, sociable twenty-something, as opposed to a jeans-and-Converse loner with an agenda bigger and more dangerous than most people's imaginations.

As I crossed Clarendon Road to cut through campus, I mentally rehearsed my story. I was meant to be an eager sixth-former deciding what institution to spend all my parents' hard-earned money on. Even though I was only interested in the chemistry department, for appearances' sake I'd booked the finance talk, the accommodation tour, the societies and clubs talk and the campus tour. My schedule for the day started at nine-thirty and ended at three-thirty – lecture in the chemistry department by Professor Molecule or whoever.

I clutched my A4 notebook and tried to get into character, which wasn't difficult. All I had to do was turn back time.

I got talking to a sweet boy from Manchester and a girl from Glasgow. I told them I was from Coventry – a random choice based on it not being either of their hometowns. We'd all booked the same morning talks so stayed as a three, eating lunch in the union building. After the finance session, we said our good-byes and I headed to the chemistry department, keen to be early for the lecture.

'I'm here for chemistry,' I said to the student at the door.

'Take a seat.' He gestured towards the empty lecture theatre.

'I'm always too early.' I shrugged. 'Are you a chemistry student?'

'Yes,' he said. Not overly chatty.

'Can you tell me a bit about it?'

He blathered on, a bit flustered and incoherent. A few more people started to arrive.

'I'd better man the doors,' he said, desperate to get rid of me.

'Yes, sorry, of course.' I paused. 'Do you think you could show me around the labs . . . maybe afterwards?'

A long pause. He didn't want to. Stupid four-eyed boffin. I'd made a bad choice. Thought he'd be flattered. Should have waited for a more confident-looking target.

'Are there any loos near here?' I asked.

He gave me directions.

The lecture theatre had doors both sides. I went the long way round and tried again.

'It's a huge room, isn't it?'

This time the geek on the door at least met my eyes.

'Chemistry's popular. A hundred and fifty students in most lectures.'

'Bit of a step up from school,' I said. Saffron seemed to have decided to be in awe.

'It doesn't feel big, not once you get to know your course.' He smiled.

We carried on the chitchat for a few minutes. I was aware of several other inquisitive types queuing to ask my guy an almost certainly pointless question.

'I'd really like to see the labs. I don't suppose you could show me?'

'I'm afraid the lecture's about to —'

'I meant afterwards.'

He didn't stop for breath. 'Sure. Why not?'

'Great,' I said, giving him a winning smile. 'I'm Saffron. See you later . . .'

The room was filling up. I left him to deal with the others and took a seat.

It was so dull, it was almost funny. Grey man. Grey suit. Powerpoint slides circa the millennium.

I feigned interest, just in case my doorman was watching me.

Forty-five minutes later the Prof handed over to one of his puppets for question time. Hands popped up all over. Mostly keeners trying to show off their knowledge:

'I'm particularly interested in supramolecular chemistry and was wondering if there is any research . . .?'

'Does the university contribute to the debate on global warming, and particularly the controversy surrounding . . .?'

(I was self-aware enough to know that my disdain was, in fact, envy. I'd never get the chance to be the know-all in the auditorium.)

When it was finally over, it took another age for me to edge along my row, because the lot coming down the aisle from the seats further back weren't letting people in.

'Samiya!'

The use of my super-dangerous forever-discarded name made my heart rate rocket. I looked down, suddenly interested in my pad of paper. It had to be a coincidence – there was obviously another girl of Arabic extraction somewhere close by. I tried to keep hold of the sound of the voice to work out if I recognised it, but my brain had shut down. Fight or flight – that was all I was capable of.

We shuffled forward agonisingly slowly. I was two people away from the aisle. Two people away from escaping. The temptation to look was overwhelming, but I resisted. If, by some incredibly bad bit of luck, it was someone who knew me, the last thing I should do was face them.

I pushed my way into the bottleneck by the entrance.

'Samiya!' It was louder this time. And definitely male.

Run. Run. Run.

Like a bull, I charged through the three-deep crowd. In the corridor there was more room to move. I dodged and weaved, walking fast. At the corner, my caution deserted me. I *had* to know.

I turned and scanned the would-be chemists.

In my panic, they all looked familiar.

I put the hood up on my cagoule and headed for home, terrified that someone from school had been in the audience.

As I turned into Brudenell Road, I forced my runaway thoughts into some sort of order. If whoever shouted my name was certain it was me, surely he wouldn't have let me slide away so easily? Everyone from Buckingham knew I was Dronejacker, a wanted criminal, so wouldn't he have called for security? Chances were he was unsure. Unsure I could deal with. In a few hours, he'd be back where he came from.

My heart rate dropped back down to seventy beats a minute, from about a zillion.

44

Freddie was obviously back – walking boots in the middle of the kitchen, sopping-wet rucksack by the back door – but out. Good. Last thing I wanted was banter. Liam had left a couple of messages. I texted back saying I was still feeling rough. I watched the news, lying on the sofa, as exhausted as if I'd run a marathon. I didn't think about what had happened, because there was no point. I couldn't abandon the plan because someone *might* have thought they recognised me.

Bed was extremely welcome.

Turned out that foolish Freddie had been on the Otley Run on Saturday night. Eighteen pubs, starting at Woodies Ale House. After three bouts of vomiting had punctuated Sunday morning, I decide to see if he was going to live.

'Do you want something for your stomach?' I asked through his door.

Groan.

'Shall I leave you alone?'

Groan.

The most I'd ever drunk was three cans of cider

with Hugo – I didn't much like the feeling. I tended to have one, to fit in, and then make it last. Bomb-makers with stolen identities and alcohol didn't sound like an ideal combination anyway. I needed to keep my wits about me at all times. Who knew what other curveballs were coming my way?

The shock of hearing someone shout my name at the lecture was waning, replaced by frustration that my lab visit had been scuppered. Without the right chemicals, I was nowhere.

For something to do, I walked to the lock-up – taking my list of names and addresses and the faces of the dead.

It was a relief, on Monday morning, to settle down to the routine tasks a customer services agent at a world-wide courier company has to perform. As usual, I made sure I didn't whizz through everything too quickly – didn't want to show up the others. At eleven, I offered to get coffees, which was just an excuse for a breath of fresh air and a chat. I didn't ask Liam. There was a kind of understanding that we lowly types were in a round together. Management had their own.

'Thanks, Saffron,' said Elisa. 'Do you want to have lunch today?'

'OK, but do you mean lunch or Topshop?'

'Lunch. But cheap.'

'Fancy a tandoori chicken flatbread?'

'Now you mention it . . .'

Before we went I had a quiet half-hour, so I typed the letter that was going to the journalists, using the words I'd been crafting in my head for weeks. I was ahead of myself, but didn't want to have to rush when it got nearer the time. I printed six, erased the document and locked the papers in my cabinet.

'Come on, then, Saff.'

I took Elisa to the café I'd taken refuge in on my first day at work. Elisa was in full flow when, like déjà vu, the round head of Dan Langley's lawyer appeared once more on the telly. I was freaked out. Fate was playing games.

I couldn't believe I'd forgotten that it was 23rd June – extradition day. The whole of the café watched in silence.

Astonishingly, the courts had decided to pack Dan off to the States. Judging by the report, it was totally unexpected. His age, his 'innocence', the fact that his actions saved the lives of Londoners, all counted for nothing versus the Americans' desire to blame someone. Dan was nowhere to be seen, but his lawyer gave a rousing speech, pledging to fight and fight.

'I feel really sorry for him,' said Elisa.

'Me too,' I said.

Elisa went back to her frame-by-frame description of Saturday night, complete with vomit, walking in bare feet on broken glass and two taxis refusing to give her a lift. I sat there wondering if Dan Langley was in a cell somewhere, regretting what he'd done to me.

'We'd better go,' she said as she mopped her plate with the last corner of flatbread. 'Don't want Liam on my back.'

She winked, which I assumed was her way of letting me know that she had suspicions about us. I didn't rise to the bait.

Bang on two o'clock we were back at the office.

What the —?

Standing in the reception of SendEx were two police officers – a woman and a familiar man with a statement moustache.

'What are they doing here?' said Elisa.

'No idea,' I said, hurrying past, head down, leaving Elisa hovering. It was uncharacteristic of me not to stop and speak to the receptionist, but I was thrown. I got to my desk, unlocked my cabinet, took out the oh-so-incriminating letters and walked to the shredder. I watched them disappear, went back to my desk and pulled some random sheets from my in-tray. The type-faces danced in front of my eyes.

Breathe, Saffron.

I'd been too complacent. Whoever it was that saw me at the lecture must have called the police. Maybe the security services had been working all weekend, cross-referencing data. I couldn't imagine how a bank account, a tax reference and an NHS number could add up to something suspicious, but what did I know? Another thought blasted its way to the surface – maybe Dan was being extradited because the Americans had new information . . . and that information somehow led to me. Was I careful enough when I bought my new identity . . .?

The possibilities charged round my body like electricity.

'This is Saffron,' said the receptionist.

I stood up and faced them.

45

'Saffron Anderson?' said the man I'd last seen in the park, aka Sergeant Collins.

'That's right,' I said.

'We've met before,' he said.

I was saying nothing until whatever *he* had to say became clear.

'We're here to follow up on a possible assault in Hyde Park on . . .' He checked the date.

I continued to look baffled, although inside I was immensely relieved that it was Maggie – and not Interpol – that had prompted the visit. I let him explain all about seeing me in the park with her, before I pretended to register what he was on about.

'Oh,' I said. 'It was nothing. We sort of tripped over each other. I think she was drunk and I was in a rush . . .'

'She's been charged with the assault of a social worker. Gave the poor woman a nasty wound. It's our duty to bring any other evidence that might help secure a conviction, such as her assault on you.'

He could huff and puff as hard as he liked, but I wasn't blowing over.

The woman police officer joined in.

'There's no need to be afraid. We could start with a statement.'

'She stumbled and I got in the way,' I said. 'That's about it.'

'That's not how I saw it,' said Sergeant Collins.

I didn't respond – easily the best way to shorten a conversation.

The woman gave me a victim-support leaflet and her card.

'If you change your mind, we're here,' she said.

'Thanks,' I said, switching my focus back to the paperwork on my desk.

I listened to them striding off. Told myself to keep things in perspective. My too-chatty flatmate must have told the too-nosy Sergeant Collins where I worked. No one suspected anything. I'd been unlucky, that was all.

I made two fists to try to stop my hands from shaking. Released them as the sound of one lot of feet receding was replaced by another set approaching.

'What was that all about?' asked Liam, unusually flustered. *Normal people don't have run-ins with the police,* I reminded myself.

I explained, making it sound very pedestrian.

'I've got to pick up my brother from Cubs again today,' he said, head bowed so that our conversation stayed private. 'Do you want to come —'

'I haven't got a leather woggle . . . or a penknife,' I said. Sad face.

'— come round to my mum and dad's after, I meant to say?'

'Sure.'

I totally got why people had affairs at work. The frisson whenever he stopped to chat totally relieved the boredom.

In between getting on with the business of the day, I went back into the Gadget Man account to check a few things, like the number of packages sent internationally, how many of those went to North America and the weight of the heaviest packages. I needn't have worried about a couple of pounds of explosive and a pressure cooker – they occasionally sent ride-on Minis that topped the scales at twenty kilograms plus. Hurrah for spoilt kids.

I checked the system and saw that we had some of their stuff going out on a van, so I popped across to the depot to have a look. I didn't want anyone who handled their goods regularly to notice anything out of the ordinary.

'Coming out on the road with me?' said one of the drivers.

'Not today, I'm afraid.'

'My loss,' he said.

There were three brown boxes – the smallest was the size of a pair of Converse, the biggest could easily have contained two pressure cookers. I checked the labels – it was all as expected.

Poor old Gadget Man was going to have to fight to clear its name once the parcels started arriving.

46

Liam's dad was a lorry driver, only home every few nights. Liam's mum was a nurse – a shift-worker, which explained Liam's weekly date picking up his brother.

'It's a job to keep track of each other,' she said, big smile, deep creases in her cheeks. 'Let alone this little scoundrel.' She tickled Liam's brother. I liked her immediately.

'Stop it, Mum,' said Luke. 'I'm not a toy.'

'That's his latest saying,' she said. 'It's better than last week's – that was, "You're not the boss of me."'

Luke stuck out his tongue.

'And Liam says you're from London.'

'That's right. Shepherd's Bush,' I said. Volunteering information is more credible than having it squeezed out of you, and gives you more control over what you say and what you don't.

'I haven't been more than half a dozen times,' she said. 'And I only ever seem to see Oxford Street.'

'Whose fault is that, Mum?' asked Liam, his arm clamped firmly round my waist.

'You can talk,' she said. 'Can't get you out of Topman.'

'Shh! I'm trying to impress Saffron.'

He grinned at me and then, to my horror, kissed me on the lips. Having never had a boyfriend (apart from the thing with Hugo), my experience of all things sexual was strictly in private. I felt a blush creep up my cheeks, despite the fact that neither Liam, his mum nor his brother seemed bothered.

'Will you come and see my badges?' said Luke, still hyper from running around doing survival skills.

'Sure,' I said.

'Tea's in ten minutes,' said Liam's mum as I followed Luke out of the door.

His room was tiny and crammed full of stuff – books, Nerf guns, Transformers . . .

My mum had wanted a boy after she'd had me, but all she got were miscarriages. Life would have been different if I'd had a brother.

'Has he bored you stupid yet?' asked Liam from the door ten minutes later.

'No. We've done the Global Conservation Activity Badge and now we're on the Collector's.' I looked at the patchwork of circles decorating his sleeve. 'I think we've got a few to go.'

'You can show her the rest next time,' said Liam, pulling me up onto my feet and propelling me along the corridor to what he called 'my old room'.

He shut the door.

'You're gorgeous,' he said, kissing my eyelids, cheeks, nose and finally lips.

'You're not bad,' I said, 'but I think I've fallen for your brother. It's all those badges . . .'

'Witch.'

Liam's mum called us down for tea before there was time to get into too much trouble.

'Can I stay at yours?' I said as we tucked in our shirts. Undercover cops were forever climbing into bed with unsuspecting women – they argued that it strengthened their cover. Sounded good to me.

'Yes, please.'

The four of us stuffed our faces with sausage and mash, followed by apple pie and custard. I don't know what it is about being fed by a mum, but there's nothing quite like it.

'Thank you very much,' I said. 'It was really tasty.'

'Anytime, Saffron. It's a treat to see Liam with a nice girl.' She raised her eyebrows.

'Why? Does he normally bring home nasty ones?'

'Yes,' said Luke. 'Chelsea was horrible.'

All three of them laughed.

'I need details,' I said.

An hour later we left to catch a bus back to Liam's flat in Headingley.

'They loved you,' said Liam.

'They're just glad I'm not Chelsea,' I said.

'So am I,' he said. 'I'm glad you're you, Saffron Anderson, the most fabulous girlfriend in . . . all of Brudenell Road.'

'Surely Queen's Road too?'

'Go on, then.'

For the next ten hours or so, I didn't give one thought to the parcels, the explosive, the detonator, the target, *Jaddah* or Lamyah. I became Saffron Anderson, Liam's girlfriend, customer services agent, kind to strays and Cubs and maker of mean French toast.

47

I left work early to visit a virtual dentist and positioned myself outside the chemistry building. I couldn't wait for another open day so was hoping to find my would-be lab guide and reschedule our tour. I bought a copy of the *Guardian* to help pass the time. Dan was on the front page, photographed with his girlfriend coming out of the courts. It was a really sweet picture, and for a second I felt sorry for him. All he'd done was be a bit too clever, and have the part of your brain that makes good decisions missing. Bit like me, some would say.

An hour and a half later, my patience was rewarded. Along came the chemist — short brown hair, maroon jumper, jeans and trainers, just like last time.

'Hi,' I said. 'We met at the open day.'

'You're the one who wanted a tour . . .'

'I'm so sorry, I had to dash. But I wondered whether we could do it another time?'

'Do you live in Leeds, then?' An entirely predictable question.

'Yes. I know it's not ideal to stay at home when you're a student, but I'm worried about the loan . . .'

'Fair enough. I'll be about fifty grand in debt by the time I leave.'

'That much?'

'I'm a post-grad, for my sins.' (I hate that expression, but smiled anyway.)

'So, would it be possible? A tour? Only I want to make the right decision.'

'It's a good course, and a good uni. Typical offer's AAB. Go for it!'

'I'm predicted A*s and As,' I said. 'My dad wants me to try for Cambridge.'

His attitude changed ever so slightly. I wasn't a good-looking girly any more, I was an *intelligent* good-looking girly.

'I was off for a drink at The Fav . . .' He looked at his watch. 'But I suppose we could do it now, if you like.'

'That's so kind. As long as you're not going to stand anyone up?' I was being hideously flirty. Someone shoot me.

'No one important,' he said with a swagger. Someone shoot him.

Clearly intent on making the most of his role as chemistry guru, he started to talk non-stop as we walked along. Suited me. I lapped it up. When he occasionally paused for breath, I asked clever questions about second-generation biofuels and the like. He looked impressed – all thanks to my seventh-hand chemistry book.

He used his ID card to get into the building and then into the lab, holding the doors for me. Someone tailgated us, but my guide didn't say anything. Security clearly not top of his agenda. He showed me the mass spectrometry equipment, the Joseph Priestley lab with its fume cupboards and the iPRD lab. I feigned interest in everything, patiently waiting to see if he would mention the storage of sensitive materials.

He did. Thorough should have been his middle name. He covered the flammable cabinets, bench storage, refrigerated storage, poisons and other substances kept under what he called 'key control'. A few well-chosen prompts had him spouting lists of chemicals kept in each location. It was almost too easy. I'd found what I was looking for without arousing a jot of suspicion. The practicalities of finding a way to rifle through the contents of the locked cupboards could wait for my next visit. I just had a couple more pieces of the puzzle to put in place.

'It's really quiet,' I said. 'I suppose that's because most of the students have gone home.'

'Not really, the undergraduates only get about nine hours' lab time. It's quiet because most post-grads and post-docs are in the pub by now!'

'So do you all work as a team?' My question sounded fake, but I needed to know whether a strange face in the lab would raise eyebrows.

'Not really a team. We work on a diverse range of projects. But there are technicians that assist.'

'But you know all the other chemists, right?'

Be careful, Saffron.

'Not at all,' he said. 'Two professors share the lab, both with large teams. I probably know less than half.'

A white-coated, goggled-up girl with a ponytail called across to a similarly dressed bloke.

'Have you got the key, Richie?'

He held it up.

'Sorry!'

'Why do you never put it back?' she said grumpily, striding past us to fetch it.

I watched her open *the* cupboard, take out a brown bottle, close it again, lock it and put the key in the third drawer of a grey metal cabinet.

'*That's* where it lives, Richie.'

Was that what the university called 'restricted access'? I made myself keep the grin inside. It was about time I had some luck.

'Doesn't anyone work through the night? You know, if they're onto something.'

'No. It's a right royal pain with security if you want to work after eight o'clock. Or at the weekend. They're like bouncers, in more ways than one.'

He smiled, pleased with his put-down. I smiled too, even though I thought he was a complete moron.

'If you've seen enough, do you want to come for a drink?' he asked, not unexpectedly – the well-groomed Saffron Anderson got a lot more attention than Samiya ever did.

No, I'd rather cut someone else's toenails.

'OK,' I said. 'I'll buy, to thank you for the tour.'

He didn't let me, insisting that it had been his pleasure. I think he was hoping for some more pleasure, but after a half of cider I said I had to go.

'If you want to know anything else, just give me a call,' he said.

I took his number, knowing I wouldn't be ringing it.

Based on what I'd seen, one visit to the lab on my tod and the three chemicals I needed – a catalyst, a depressant and a primer, to ensure the bomb exploded rather then fizzed – would be in the lock-up with the rest of the components. Good job.

Back at Freddie's, there was a copy of *Metro* on the kitchen table with a familiar face on the front page.

No way!

One day and everything had changed. Slippery Dan Langley wasn't going to be extradited after all because the American government had withdrawn its request. Good. No extradition meant no court case. No court case meant Dronejacker got archived with the rest of yesterday's news.

Until the next time . . .

For a second I allowed myself to imagine the day when the Americans finally acknowledged that firing missiles at innocent people had consequences. *Major* consequences. It was electrifying.

I reined in the feeling. It was dangerous to focus

too much on the prize. It wouldn't happen unless the planning was meticulous. And this time, no loose ends.

48

The plan was complete in that I understood how to get everything I needed to make the bomb, how to parcel it, how to send it and to whom, and how to detonate it. But I still didn't have enough ammonium nitrate. So I went foraging three lunchtimes running, telling Elisa I was looking for a present for her birthday.

Just before I left work on Friday evening, I typed the warning letters again, printed them and put them in my rucksack together with seventeen cold packs from the little cabinet under my desk. I got a bus to the lock-up, entered the code for the main door and went in, glancing up at the CCTV as I walked along to my unit.

I took out my key and let myself in, shutting the door behind me and locking it. I emptied the rucksack, putting the cold packs with all the others and the letters in my file. I was keen to get home in time for a bath because Liam and I were going clubbing. But I didn't leave straight away. I sat on the pressure cooker that was still in its box and leafed through my notes. In theory there was nothing to stop the bomb from flying over the Atlantic in the next two weeks. Being so close, for the second time, evoked conflicting feelings.

I didn't want to think about leaving Leeds. Never seeing Liam again, or Mack and Elisa . . . even Freddie. Having mates and being Liam's girlfriend was nice, but it could never be enough — I needed closure. Recognition that cold-blooded murder had consequences.

Starting again would be Strange, capital S. What would I do? I had no plans to become a career activist. As soon as the world recognised that the drone wars were illegal, irresponsible, indefensible, my job would be over and —

There was a tap on the door. I froze. People weren't meant to come calling. I checked the time. Six-fifteen.

'Yes?' I shouted.

'It's Alan, the manager.'

I didn't care who it was. The door was staying shut.

'Hi,' I shouted.

'Can I have a word?'

No.

'OK.' I opened the door just wide enough to slide out.

'Afternoon,' said the bloke I recognised from before — pale and skinny with an attractive blend of body odour and fags.

'Hi,' I said again.

'Still stockpiling?' he said.

'Yes, there's a way to go.'

I'd told him I was studying art and design at the college and needed the space to collect materials for an installation based on flight. It explained my frequent comings and goings with different-sized bits and bobs.

'There's an offer,' he said. 'Thought you might be interested.'

'I'm listening.'

He outlined the deal – if I moved upstairs, I could have a month's extension free of charge.

'I'm happy here,' I said.

'Thing is,' he said, 'I've got a customer who wants three units next to each other on the ground floor.'

'I really can't move,' I said. 'There are pieces of work half finished, and stuff gluing . . .'

'I could help you move,' he said.

I should have gone to Big Yellow. It was bigger, more anonymous, not run by Alan.

'I'm sorry.' I turned away and attempted to disappear back inside. He rammed his steel-capped boot into the gap so I couldn't shut the door.

'Miss . . . Anderson, isn't it? Listen —'

He leant forward. I had no idea how much he could see. Thanks to the Boston bomber, even a moron would realise I was up to no good if they saw the pressure cookers.

'Take your foot out of the way,' I said, with more confidence than I felt.

'No need to get antsy,' he said. 'I just —'

We both heard the tapping of the digits on the entry pad and the main door crank open. Alan turned to see who it was. I took advantage of the slight movement and pushed him.

'I've got to get on.'

He tipped backwards and I slammed the door, immediately locking it.

Phew!

He uttered something uncomplimentary, then turned his attention to the person who'd let himself in. I couldn't catch all the words, but it sounded like he was offering them the same deal. I took a few deep breaths, talking to myself as I did so. I needed to make sure Alan understood that my contents couldn't be disturbed, just in case he got any ideas that I was a drug dealer or harbouring asylum seekers. I slipped out of the door and walked towards the two of them.

'Don't worry, *Miss* Anderson,' said Alan. 'This *gentleman*'s agreed to move, so your flappy birds or whatever are safe in there.'

'I'm sorry, but it's my art,' I said in a lovey voice. 'It's very precious to me.'

'Looked like a pile of saucepans to me,' said Alan.

Despite my instinct telling me to let it go – his voice had no hint of suspicion – I said, 'I use them for glue. Saucepans with handles are much easier to hold than bowls.'

'Get sodding Picasso here,' he said.

I left Alan and the *gentleman* laughing, wishing I'd factored in the bombing of a storage facility in Leeds.

49

Liam and I went to The Warehouse. My first ever nightclub! Going straight from eighteen to twenty-one meant I'd missed out on the social life that usually starts when you get legit ID. I was absurdly excited.

He could dance really well, and somehow his rhythm infected me. A typically English rosy-cheeked girl was watching us, and it took a while to realise that it wasn't because we looked odd, but because we looked good. I'd thrown on a bright-red skater dress with bare legs and ankle boots and somehow that worked. Liam was, as always, kitted out like a model for Next. We had a couple of drinks, and then Liam had a couple more, but I was wary of being out of control.

It was late when we left the club, and Liam was tired and emotional.

'Why can't I ever come to yours?' he asked.

'Because I live in a hovel with an idiot.'

'Come live with me,' he said, wrapping his arms around me.

The first I knew of Saturday was the smell of bacon. Delicious. I yanked back the stripy duvet and pulled on one of Liam's T-shirts that I found on the floor – it said 'Free the Bears'.

'Free them from what?' I asked, padding into the kitchen-diner-lounge, which was the only other room in his studio flat.

'They're kept in horrible conditions, with catheters stuffed in their gall bladders to milk the bile.'

I made an appropriately disgusted face. He kissed it.

'What the hell do they do that for?'

'They use it in traditional medicine – like they use rhino horn. Witch-doctor stuff!'

He did a weird jig, which was clearly meant to be a dance to the gods of Mumbo Jumbo.

'Is this what you're like with a hangover?'

'No. This is me being happy,' he said, and then rugby-tackled me onto the chequerboard lino.

Children with no brothers and sisters don't get to wrestle. I liked it.

I should have gone home, bought more cold packs and taken them to the lock-up, but I didn't. I stayed at Liam's. Saturday merged into Sunday and before I knew it we were getting a bus to his parents' for Sunday lunch – Liam was keen for me to meet his dad.

We sat on the top deck at the front, like kids. My head on Liam's shoulder.

After he'd given me the run-down on his extended family, he said, 'Can I ask about your family?'

'Nothing to say,' I said. An image of my mum waiting for me to come out of school, a smile at the ready, appeared in sharp focus. If I could have magicked myself back to being eight, I would have.

'What happened?' he said.

'I don't want to talk about it.'

'Saffron, we've got close, haven't we? You can tell me. I'd like to know.'

I was comfortable, pressed against him. It would have been easy to invent some story – an abusive father, a messy divorce with stepsiblings – but I didn't want to lie to him at that minute. I wanted to tell him that I had a family every bit as loving as his . . .

'Not now,' I said.

He left it, of course, because Liam was a genuinely nice guy, involved with someone he knew nothing about.

I was usually good at blocking things out that weren't helpful, but as the bus trundled along the streets of Leeds, all I could think about was how Liam made me feel.

Happy.

For so long I'd been like Spock, machine-like, focused on the job, plotting all the time, watching my back, never relaxed, never content . . .

'What are you thinking?' said Liam.

Good question.

'That I'm happy,' I said.

He looked like I'd presented him with a Porsche

911, wrapped up in a silver bow. My heart did something out of character. So out of character I couldn't find a word for it. But I had a word for what came next. Guilt — because he thought what we had was real, and I knew it wasn't.

He kissed me, and I concentrated on that instead. It was easier.

Liam's brother was waiting for us, standing on the wall outside their house wearing an absolutely filthy T-shirt.

'Hiya, Saffron.'

'Hi there, Luke,' I said.

'No, she doesn't want to come and see your Lego,' said Liam.

'I might do,' I said.

'You don't,' said Liam.

'I don't want to show her my Lego,' said Luke. 'I want to show her my robot. Are you coming, Saffron?'

'OK,' I said, suddenly in no hurry to meet Liam's dad. What the hell was I doing, getting all cosied up with Liam's family when in a few weeks I'd be gone? Would I end up wrecking his family? Like those undercover cops.

Stop it, Saffron.

There was no point dwelling on the casualties of my plans — they were the price. I cleared my head and concentrated on Luke's fabulous robot.

It was as tall as Luke, made entirely of junk, and

standing upright thanks to a string suspended from the ceiling of his bedroom.

'It's brilliant,' I said.

'It's for my Artist's Badge.'

His step-by-step explanation of 'the build' took us up to dinnertime.

'Here's the mystery girl,' said Liam's dad, hand outstretched.

I shook it.

'Hello, Mr —'

'Frank,' he said.

Frank was large round the middle. He also had a large face, a large smile and a large glass of beer, as did Liam.

'Can I get you a glass of wine?' he asked.

'Yes, please,' I said, even though most wine tasted like salad dressing. It was funny to think how much of my life I'd spent doing what I thought people wanted me to, rather than what *I* wanted.

We went through into the dining room where the table was laid for five.

'You'd think the Queen was visiting,' said Frank. 'It's usually a tray in front of the telly.'

'He's joking,' said Liam's mum. 'He's not funny, but he tries. Bless him.'

It was nice, listening to the chat, spotting the similarities between the four of them, and a treat to have another home-cooked meal. The potatoes were crunchy, the meat was carved in thick slices and there was a vat of gravy. I stuffed myself. And then the conversation, which had trickled along quite nicely, shifted.

'Where are your folks, then, Saffron?' asked Frank.

'I don't see them,' I said.

'Are they abroad?' he asked, missing the point.

'No,' I said. 'We fell out.'

'That's a shame,' said Liam's mum.

'Where did they come from, then?' asked Liam's dad, determined to establish my provenance.

Liam rolled his eyes.

'I'm half Spanish,' I said.

'We love Spain. Don't we, Luke?'

'Is that where the water park was?'

Everyone laughed. A perfect moment to move on, but . . .

'You know, Saffron, everyone round here used to be English, but now you can't turn a corner without bumping into a mosque.'

'Don't start, Frank,' said Liam's mum. She turned to me and said, 'I'm sorry. He can't get used to the fact that we've had a few Muslims move into the street.'

'God knows why so many of them want to live here if they hate us.'

'Dad, you're being ignorant,' said Liam. '*They* don't hate us. In fact, there is no "they". Muslims, Jews, Buddhists – they're like you and me.'

Frank didn't like that one bit.

'Tell that to the victims of 7/7,' said Frank. 'Could have been any one of us. Incinerated.'

Incinerated like my grandma and Lamyah.

The word was like a switch, turning on my memories of the clear skies above the village in Yemen, the sound of the adhan calling people to the mosque, the taste of the hot peppery sauce, the smiles of the people.

'Don't take any notice of him, Saffron. He's miffed because the pub's closing and an application's been put in for an Islamic learning centre.'

'My dad used to go to that pub,' said Frank.

'He used to get thrown out as well,' said Liam, going on to tell a funny story about his granddad. Evidently he lived till he was eighty-nine.

Lucky man.

50

Monday was a new start.

Liam's dad had done me a favour – reminding me that there were people who thought every Muslim was desperate to slip on a suicide vest. It was his kind of attitude that had set me on my path. Dad's family were Muslims, living in Yemen – that was all the excuse the drone pilot needed.

At lunchtime, despite Liam's pleas, I said I had shopping to do and went on a serious cold-pack hunt. There was a balance between not wanting to raise any suspicions, and my amassing of them being so slow that I'd be a grandma myself before I had enough for a decent bomb.

At three o'clock Liam brought me over a cup of peppermint tea.

'Saffron, I know you said you're not cross, but —'

'Don't do this at work,' I said.

He was worried his dad would come between us. In time he'd realise that what was going to come between us was a lot worse than some politically incorrect opinions.

'Come for a drink, then? After work.'

'Tomorrow,' I said. 'Let's go to the cinema – after I've cooked for my undernourished housemates.'

'All right.'

He smiled, showing his perfect teeth. If only Mum could see what a nice chap I'd bagged. That was one of the many things that hurt – knowing that my first eighteen years would always remain separate from what came after. My mind was threatening to dredge up her face . . . her kissing Liam on the cheek . . . saying he was a lovely boy . . .

Stop it.

I hadn't seen Mum for twelve and a half weeks. Instead of being angry with her, like I was when I left, I'd started to remember the nice things – teaching me to swim and going for hot chocolate afterwards, wet hair stuck to our heads . . . making flowers out of tissue paper and pipe cleaners . . . laughing at *Miranda*.

It was like the drone strike had coloured everything in my life, stopping me from seeing properly.

I tried to imagine living a normal life with yet another identity, but it wouldn't take shape. I painted a mental picture of a little cottage in rural Scotland. I enrolled myself on a course, gave myself a bike and a boyfriend – but he looked just like Liam.

Elisa stopped by my desk, interrupting my unsatisfactory daydream.

'Saffron, I'm having a party,' said Elisa. 'Friday night. You *have* to come.'

'Thanks,' I said. Even if you're pretending to be

someone else, it's still nice to be liked. 'I'll come if I can.'

'You'd better,' she said. 'My parents have just told me they're going away, so as far as I'm concerned it's an all-nighter. Saturday's hangover day and Sunday's clear-up. Shall I invite Liam?'

'Up to you,' I said.

'We all *know*,' she said.

'Still up to you.'

By Friday I was ready for a party.

I'd been shopping every day, either at lunchtime or after work or both, and bought loads of cold packs and a bright-blue dress.

I'd cooked chicken fajitas for Polly and Freddie.

I'd bumped into Mack and ended up buying him some athlete's foot cream and a new pair of trainers because his skin was all peely.

I'd been to the storage unit twice – once to offload the contents of my overflowing cabinet and a range of flattened cardboard boxes from the depot, and the second time, in a taxi, with four quadcopters.

There'd been two drone strikes, one in Pakistan, one in Yemen. Death toll – fifteen.

Liam and I had been out twice – the cinema and the pub.

I'd shouted out in my sleep. According to Liam it sounded like, 'Don't shoot.'

I'd had my first appraisal with the team leader and

been offered a permanent contract. (And cried in the loos afterwards – which I'd put down to tiredness.)

I'd like to have left the office early and had a long soak before getting ready, but I had stuff under my desk *and* one last job to tick off before the weekend. So I went to Alan's storage facility *again* in a taxi *again*.

I arrived at twenty to six.

'I owe the owner next month's money,' I said to the driver, 'but I won't have it until Monday and he can be a bit nasty, so do you mind if we wait till he comes out?'

'I hope you've got enough for the cab,' he said, deadpan, so I couldn't tell if he was joking.

'I have if you make it a fiver,' I said.

He turned round with a smile on his big red face.

'The price is the price, cheeky madam.'

Just then Alan walked out of the door, got into his pick-up and drove away. All clear.

I paid the proper price, six quid, and asked the cabbie to pick me up in an hour. He gave me his card.

Inside my rucksack and three opaque plastic bags, I had twenty-seven cold packs, a large granite mortar and pestle and a mini quadcopter, which I stacked on top of the others. It was time to start grinding. Once I knew how long it took to turn the beads from the cold packs into powder, I could plan when to filch the controlled substances from the university. I didn't want to take them too early in case someone noticed they were missing and raised the alarm. Keeping the spot-light off Leeds until I got away was critical.

I sat on the pressure-cooker box with the mortar on my lap and filled it with beads. At first, the pestle kept slipping, but I soon developed a better technique. Even then, it took a while to achieve a nice powder. To make a mixture that easily ignited I needed uniformity, and I didn't need impurities. I worked at it for nearly an hour, grinding up four separate batches that I tipped into two pristine Kilner jars. My elbow felt like I'd been returning Nadal's serves, so I shut up shop. After all, there was a driver waiting, and I had a party to go to.

Freddie was in the kitchen with a mate.

'Hey, Saff! I'm making risotto – want some?'

I peered into the saucepan. It looked like porridge.

'I'd rather try my luck in the bins,' I said, because Freddie expected banter. His mate laughed.

'We're going to the Brudenell —'

'Social Club. No, thanks,' I said.

'Saff thinks a good night out is the Hyde Park Picture House,' Freddie said to his sidekick.

'Actually, I'm going to a party in Chapel Allerton.'

'With your sugar daddy?' asked Freddie.

I made a pained expression.

'He's my boss, not my pimp.'

For no particular reason I stayed chatting, rather than disappearing up the stairs like normal.

'So whose party is it?' asked Freddie.

'No one you know.'

'Try me.'

'Elisa Sullivan – she's like me but more senior.'

They wanted to know all about her, so I made up a load of rubbish to amuse them.

'She celebrates her cat's birthday.'

'She has vodka and orange on her muesli.'

Actually, that one wasn't so far from the truth.

'I think you should come with us instead,' said Freddie, dishing out his stomach-lining rice dish. 'She sounds like a bad influence.'

'I'll pass,' I said. 'Have a good evening.'

I heard them go out about an hour later. Polly was with her boyfriend in Birmingham as usual, so I had the place to myself. Nice. I had a bath, sprayed with Dettol first, and then slipped on the sleeveless bodycon dress I'd bought especially. Ten minutes later, slap on my face and perfume everywhere else, I was on my way to meet Liam.

He was waiting on the corner of Hyde Park.

'You look fantastic,' he said.

'So do you,' I said.

He tried to take a photo of us on his phone, but I put my hand over my face.

'I'm taking a stand against vanity,' I said. 'On behalf of all ugly people.'

He laughed.

We got the bus, arriving suitably late. The house

was jam-packed. Someone shoved a bottle in my hand. We pressed our way through the crowded hall and found a few people from work in the sitting room. The music was deafening. Good deafening. We danced. We drank. We danced. Being a chameleon was a strain. Humans can only take so much. I'd had enough. For once, I was letting go. I emptied my head, and filled it with alcohol.

And then Freddie arrived with his mate.

'Hey, Saff!'

I was an idiot. It never occurred to me, despite the questioning, that he'd gatecrash. My drunken brain ran through the many downsides of Freddie meeting Liam — by which time they'd already met.

'I'm the flatmate. I assume you're the —'

'Boyfriend,' I said, to avoid Freddie saying *pimp*.

'Great. Let's swap notes,' said Freddie. 'The Saffron I know has no past. What's that all about?'

51

Liam and Freddie were having a great time, playing with the idea that I had a shady background. It was excruciating, but I had to pretend it was a lark.

'I'm going for a Saudi Arabian princess, loaded, but determined to experience the life of a pauper,' said Freddie.

'No. Found in a basket, hidden in the bulrushes – raised by moorhens,' said Liam, a bit slurred.

'Like Thumbelina?' asked Freddie.

'I was thinking Moses,' said Liam.

They laughed some more.

Elisa, who'd been hovering behind Freddie, joined in. 'She's an avatar.'

'Genetically modified,' added Freddie, slinging an arm around her.

It was all going horribly wrong. Not only was it a matter of time before someone suggested something near the truth, but Freddie and Elisa were looking altogether too interested in each other. I really didn't want my work life and my home life to merge. Freddie would pounce on the tiniest inconsistency.

'Or in witness protection,' said Freddie.

It was Weird, capital W, hearing Freddie say the same words I'd said to Hugo.

Things were getting out of control and I wasn't doing anything about it.

'Or a secret agent,' said Liam.

I pulled his sleeve, swaying slightly.

'Liam, let's get some fresh air. I don't feel well.'

He followed me out into the back garden.

'Freddie's a laugh,' he said.

'He's all right,' I said.

'Why *don't* we ever go to yours?'

'Because it's not mine. It's Freddie's.' My tone was uncharacteristically stern.

A couple of other people from work spilled out of the back door and came to join us.

'I didn't know you two were an item,' said the girl from reception.

'Everyone knows,' said the bloke from accounts.

'Well, I didn't,' she said.

'That's because keeping secrets is Saff's speciality,' said Freddie, lurching out of the door towards us, his hand in Elisa's.

He was like a dog with a bone. I knew why. It was being estranged from my family – he wanted the story. He had no idea who I really was, but I still needed him to shut up. If anyone looked too closely beneath the sophistication, they might just spot a possibly half-Yemeni girl of anything between eighteen and twenty-five, and where might that thought go?

You have to take control of a situation.

Come on, Saffron.

'Not everyone has the perfect family, Freddie,' I said, my voice deliberately shaky to show I was being made to say something. 'It was my choice to leave mine behind. And my choice not to share the reasons with you.'

As I hoped, that took the wind out of his sails.

'See you on Monday,' I said to Elisa as I grabbed Liam's hand and headed for the little alley that ran down the side of the house.

'I didn't mean anything, Saff,' said Freddie, talking to my back. 'It was just a bit of fun.'

I was reminded of Hugo again, and his bit of fun in the common room.

Liam stopped, turned round and said, 'Leave it, Freddie. It's gone too far.'

I carried on through the side gate and waited by the smelly wheelie bin.

'OK, OK,' I heard Freddie say. 'There's no need to overreact. I wasn't suggesting she was a terrorist or anything.'

There was the unmistakable sound of a fist hitting a face, and then Liam strode out of the alley rubbing his knuckles.

'Please can we go,' I said, desperate for the evening to be over. It was a mistake to have got involved with Liam, a mistake to have dropped my guard with Freddie, a mistake to have even gone to the party.

No more mistakes.

52

We got home at about two and went straight to sleep, but I woke a couple of hours later. Alcohol alters your brain chemistry – in my case it made me paranoid. Afraid that I was leaving clues without realising. Afraid that another Dan Langley might trip me up. Afraid that I wasn't sure what to be afraid of.

I slipped out of bed, got dressed and let myself out of Liam's flat.

The walk home took half an hour. I passed drunks, couples snogging, townies, students, several cats and a fox. Realising the sun was about to rise, I carried on into Hyde Park and sat for a while on the slide – Mack's favourite spot. It was the beginning of July. I'd been in Leeds since the beginning of April. Three months of procrastinating. You can lie to other people, but you must never lie to yourself. If I'd wanted to, I could have had the whole thing done and dusted, but I'd chosen to drag my heels. There was no law against enjoying yourself, but I hadn't sacrificed my chance of an education, my family, the right to live without fear, the possibility of ever being loved by someone who knew who I really was, to live as

Saffron Anderson. I hadn't left Samiya behind just to be someone else.

There was no going back, which meant the only way was forward.

I went home, showered away the toxins of the night before, got dressed and left Freddie a note.

Really sorry Liam took a swing at you.
Please don't make me homeless.
    Saff

I bought a coffee in town and walked to the storage unit. It was a lovely day, but that didn't lift my mood. I ground the rest of the beads, making three Kilner jars in all. Time to decorate the quadcopters. I glued a photo onto each one and wrote the name of the innocent victim, and the date they were killed.

I put them in six plain cardboard boxes, following the guidelines for packing devices with batteries.

At twelve-thirty, aching from being hunched over, I left the unit and went to find some food. I bought falafel with some mix of tahini, beetroot, salad and salsa. Thought about how I asked Mum to stop giving me falafel in my lunchbox because Lucy had cheese sandwiches. What a waste of a childhood, to be so concerned with fitting in.

I reluctantly went back to the sequence of tasks written on a list inside my head.

Letters.

I read the words I'd crafted, hoping they did the job.

> ... American drones carrying Hellfire missiles kill indiscriminately. The victims are denied the right to defend themselves, denied justice, denied a voice. Their families are denied any acknowledgement, explanation, apology or compensation.
>
> The human right to live without fear applies to all, but today the fear has switched from tribal areas of Somalia, Pakistan, Afghanistan and Yemen to somewhere near you. Sleep tight. Because tomorrow there'll be an act of retribution that will make America think twice about the unlawful war it continues to wage on innocents of all ages.

The international community had the power to stop the drone wars, they just needed to be given a reason. I had my reason. I wanted the little girl with the big brown eyes, whose face haunted me, to play outside on sunny days before her childhood disappeared.

I signed each letter 'Dronejacker', folded the six sheets and put them in envelopes before placing them on top of the bubble-wrapped quadcopters.

I checked my phone. I had four missed calls from Liam and one from Elisa. I didn't listen to my messages, or return any of them. I sat on my pressure-cooker box and tried, not for the first time, to think about what came next. I had money, and I had another dead girl's name (although training myself to answer to Georgia was a big ask), but I couldn't make it real. The idea of a winter hidden away in the Scottish Highlands felt like make-believe.

I stood up suddenly and had that funny dizzy feeling. This time next week, Saffron Anderson would be back where she belonged – in the ground. Once I'd got what I needed from the chemistry lab on Monday, there was nothing to stop me sending all the parcels on Tuesday – with the quadcopters scheduled to arrive on Wednesday and the bomb scheduled to arrive on Thursday. My eyes prickled with tears, but I didn't cry.

53

My messages were – Liam wanting to know where I was, and Elisa wanting to tell me that Freddie was currently pressure-washing vomit off her drive and that he was marvellous and they were going to have a night in with a takeaway and she was deliriously happy, all without a breath.

I called Liam on the way home, fake jolly.

'I don't know about you, but my head has only just stopped thumping,' I said.

'I was worried, Saffron.' Liam sounded a bit out of breath. 'You could have left a note.'

'I left in a hurry. Didn't want to throw up in your flat.'

'You can throw up in my flat any day. What you can't do is disappear without a trace.'

Gulp.

'Isn't that a line from *CSI*?'

'No, it's a line from me, your lovely boyfriend.'

I stopped walking, momentarily lost for words. Two joggers nearly ran into me.

'Where are you?' I asked.

'Where are you?' he said.

'In the park,' I said. 'About to get mown down by joggers.'

Another over-keen runner was coming up behind me, so I stepped onto the grass to let him pass.

Two arms, hot and bare, grabbed me, nearly knocking me off balance.

I screamed. Loud.

'Shhh!!' said Liam, 'I'll get arrested.'

'Idiot!' I said, burying my head in his chest. His running vest was wet. The tears I'd been storing up took advantage of the shock and mingled with his sweat.

'What's wrong?' he asked the top of my head.

There was no answer to that, so I stayed where I was while he kissed my hair, his breath as humid as the wind that met me in Yemen.

'Saffron, what's up?'

He stepped away an inch so he could tip my chin up and see me, but I couldn't look at him. He'd done nothing wrong, yet he was going to be collateral damage.

I managed to squeeze out the words, 'Tired and emotional'.

He took my hand and walked me home.

'Coming in?' I asked at the door. Where was the harm? After all, our time was nearly up.

'I don't smell too lovely,' he said.

I ran him a bath, but it went cold.

Tomorrow never comes. There's only ever now. I made Liam's now as nice as I possibly could.

54

For me, Monday started at two-thirty in the morning. I was glad to be awake, because my dreams were exhausting. Knowing that sleep would only bring more scenes of carnage, punctuated by episodes from my past and present that had never happened but seemed real, I got up and made a mug of tea. It was raining. A steady drizzle by the sound of it. Matched my mood.

I thought about writing a letter to Liam, but what would I say?

No one writes letters any more. They write emails and cards and texts. Mum kept a box of old letters. They were dead boring, but she loved reading them out loud to me. Some of them were from her to her mum, sent when she went to Southend-on-Sea with her aunty.

We went swimming in the sea. It was freezing. We had a hot chocolate afterwards. Aunty said I had a cocoa moustache.

I guess she just liked having something from her past.

I left my mug in the sink and went back upstairs. The only thing I had from my past was the photo. I took it out of my purse.

If only . . .

Don't go there, Samiya.

I was at my desk by eight o'clock, keen to busy my mind. The team leader arrived twenty minutes later.

'You don't have to work any harder now you're permanent,' she said. 'Elisa'll be calling you names again.'

'Couldn't sleep,' I said.

She disappeared over to the other side of the office.

Liam arrived next. Freshly shaven, tanned face, pale-blue shirt – the sort of guy who should have a sweet, innocent girlfriend.

'Hi, early bird.'

'Who are you calling a bird?' I said.

'Sorry. Good morning, Ms Anderson.'

'That's more like it.'

He, after a quick glance round the office, pecked me on the cheek.

'Come with me to get Luke from Cubs tonight, will you?'

'I can't —'

'Dad won't be home.'

'I'm not avoiding your dad, Liam. I need to do some washing and —'

'At it already, lovebirds?'

It was Elisa, looking incredibly tired. Liam sidled off.

'Thanks for the party,' I said.

'Thanks for bringing you know who,' she said.

'I didn't bring him. He gatecrashed.'

She spent the morning asking me all about Freddie.

'Considering you live with him, you don't seem to know much about him,' she said, frustrated that she couldn't read his horoscope because I didn't know when his birthday was.

'I do. He likes bacon and getting wasted, and has posh parents. What else is there?'

'He said more or less the same about you,' she said.

'I'm all ears . . .'

'Definitely got secrets, brilliant cook, no parents, good-looking . . .' She stopped to see my reaction.

'Obviously,' I said.

'But scary.'

I let that one go.

'Was he livid about Liam?' I asked.

'Not really. He knew he was being an arse.'

At lunchtime she dragged me to Primark, Topshop, Oasis, New Look and Zara, looking for something to wear to the pub. I didn't see what was wrong with jeans and a T-shirt, but Elisa's idea of casual was anything but.

I went through the motions – pretending to care that the red polka dot was too tight under the arms. My only objective was to get through the day.

At four o'clock, having blitzed through all my work,

I went into the Gadget Man account and input the details of the seven parcels. SendEx drivers picked up Gadget Man packages from either the store itself or their warehouse. I used Liam's password to add another approved pick-up point – a mini-supermarket near the office that took drop-offs. I'd been there with Elisa to return some ASOS purchases.

The next job was to ensure that the six quadcopters all arrived at around the same time, despite the wild variations in distance. I had to pay extra to get Next-Day Delivery Guaranteed for the ones that had furthest to travel. Or rather, Gadget Man did. Scheduling the bomb to arrive twenty-four hours after the rest was easy.

I'd just finished printing off the labels and the accompanying documentation when Liam came along. I rested my elbow on the pile of papers.

'Sure you don't want to come and talk reef knots with my brother?'

'Tempting . . . but no.'

'Tomorrow night, then?'

'It's my night to cook,' I said. 'Wednesday?'

'You're on.'

I put the papers into my rucksack.

I went to the lock-up, dumped the paperwork, grabbed my white lab coat and caught a bus to the university. The sun had dried up all the rain, so I sat cross-legged on the grass, bang opposite the entrance to the chemistry department. I was dreading the next couple of hours. Theft wasn't my area of expertise, but without the chemicals from the locked cupboard, there'd be no bang.

At twenty-five to six, my lab guide left the building and walked towards The Fav. Satisfied that he'd gone for the day, and therefore there'd be no one to recognise me, I went to the union to kill time. I wanted the labs to be empty, so that meant waiting until close to eight o'clock – any later and security would get involved.

I bought chips and a pint of blackcurrant squash, and read a copy of *Metro*. The minutes went by excruciatingly slowly.

By seven, I was in such a state that waiting any longer was counter-productive. I walked from the union to the chemistry building, swiped Polly's card ... and nothing happened.

No!

Polly must have finally got around to reporting her card missing.

A young guy was right behind me.

Snap decisions.

'Excuse me, I'm so stupid. I've got the wrong —'

'No problem,' he said, holding the door for me. He glanced at my face. My mind fast-forwarded to his inevitable witness interview ...

I dived into the loos to put on the white coat and then strolled along to the lab with my rucksack on my back.

Act like you own the place.

It was empty. I put my rucksack on the floor, took out some papers and scattered them on the work surface. I went over to the metal cabinet with a pen in my hand. I opened the third drawer down and took out the key. I heard voices in the corridor.

Ignore them.

I went across to the locked cupboard, used the key to open it and quickly scanned the labels. The words danced. The voices got louder.

I shut my eyes, calling up the visual memory of the names of the compounds I needed.

Concentrate, Saffron.

I read the label twice before taking the bottle I needed out of the cupboard and slipping it into my pocket. Two girls walked into the lab, chatting away. I pushed the cupboard door to and walked back to where I'd left my rucksack. I concentrated on nothing. My hand made shapes on the page.

Five minutes passed, but it seemed like fifty. The girls finished whatever it was they were doing by the fume cupboards. As they went to leave, one of them turned to look at me.

'Make sure you lock that one and put the key back or you'll be in big trouble.'

They both laughed.

'I will,' I said, my heart banging in my chest.

They left the lab

I went back to the cupboard containing the restricted

chemicals and, starting again at the top shelf, studied each word on every label as if it were a hieroglyphic.

As I took the second and third bottles, knowing there was now nothing standing between me and an explosion on American soil, my knees almost buckled.

Don't think.

I locked the cupboard and replaced the key in the cabinet drawer. On the side there was a long metal spatula asking to be taken. I slipped it in my rucksack, together with the papers.

Back in the ladies, I scrumpled up the white coat and shoved that in too.

The plan was to go back to the storage unit, but I couldn't face it. Storing the chemicals in my room overnight was hardly going to foil the whole plot.

I walked back through the park, as on edge as if the bomb itself was on my back.

'Saff!'

'Hello, Mack.' Instant cheery voice. 'How's things?'

'All right,' he said. He was wearing new clothes.

'Been shopping?' I asked.

'Mum got them.'

'Nice.'

'She's going to college,' he said.

'Your mum?'

According to Mack, whose stories rarely made sense, the social worker that his mum had assaulted had helped her enrol on a hair and beauty course.

'I've been to school too,' he said.

'That's brilliant,' I said.

'Not today,' he said, clearly a bit overwhelmed by my enthusiasm. 'But I might go tomorrow.'

'What's going to decide you?'

'The weather,' he said.

I turned my palms upwards to signify a lack of understanding.

'Don't want to be outside if it's too hot. Might burn my neck again.'

Fair enough.

'I'd go if I were you,' I said. 'Might learn something.'

'What?' he said. 'Can we have an ice cream?'

I bought him a Cornetto.

'See you, then, Mack,' I said as we reached Hyde Park Road.

'Is that man who runs your boyfriend?' he asked, in his typically random fashion.

'Yes,' I said. I'd noticed Mack had a knack for remembering faces, which was lucky given that he couldn't recognise letters. It's good to have some talents.

'I like him. He gives me money,' said Mack. 'Fiver, every time.'

He ran off.

I walked down Brudenell Avenue, wishing I could turn back time.

55

I was at the storage unit by six in the morning on Tuesday, which gave me at least two hours before Alan was due to arrive. Didn't want to risk him jamming his steel toecaps in the door to offer me *another* discount.

The only way I could even begin to make the explosive was by imagining it was a cake. I added each ingredient to the bucket I'd bought from Wilko and stirred, slowly and carefully, using the stainless-steel spatula. When the mixture looked uniform, I packed it tightly into one of the second-hand pressure cookers – chosen at random from the three. Attaching the phone was a bit fiddly, so I ended up taping it onto the handle. With the cooker bubble-wrapped as though it were Swarovski crystal, I turned the phone on and sealed the box. Knowing that all I had to do was ring or text the number and it would explode was both terrifying and unbelievable. I had to resist the urge to try it out, like people with vertigo who lean over balconies.

I attached the labels and the paperwork to each of the seven parcels. There for all to see were the details of the sender, Gadget Man, and the recipient, a description of the contents and the warning about the lithium battery. In the see-through docket were the customs documents and the invoice.

I left the pile of boxes in the centre and locked up.

On the way into work, I rang the same taxi driver that I'd used before and arranged for him to pick me up round the corner from SendEx at twelve-thirty-five.

If I'd thought the day before was bad, Tuesday was a thousand times worse. I struggled to act normally. The coffee in my cup slopped over the edge. My fingers couldn't type. And unless I hooked my feet round the legs of my chair, my whole lower body fidgeted.

'Are you ill?' asked Elisa. 'Or on drugs?'

'Neither,' I said, and then thought better of it. 'I might have a temperature.'

'Don't come near me, then.'

I kept my head down, pretending to work. A hand on my shoulder made me flinch.

'Steady,' said Liam, 'or HR'll accuse me of harassment.'

'I was thinking,' I said.

He sat on the edge of my desk, relaxed and happy. I was the opposite.

'About me?' he asked.

I nodded. Normally I'd have made some sort of quip. But my wit and humour were off sick.

'You all right?'

'Absolutely,' I said. 'But I'd better get on.' It was an entirely fake conversation.

Bang on twelve-thirty, I left the office.

'Can you take me to the storage unit on Kirkstall Road to get some boxes and then drop me and them off in town?'

'Got any money today?' asked the driver.

'Of course.'

'It'll be my pleasure, then.'

There wasn't much traffic, so minutes later we were there.

I jumped out of the taxi and was about to put in the entry code when the door opened. It was Alan, with a cigarette in his mouth and a lighter at the ready.

'Hello,' I said.

'If it isn't Picasso,' he said, before looking over at the taxi. 'That yours?'

'I'm just picking up some . . . pieces I've made that are going to be exhibited. They're boxed up.'

'Need a hand?' he said.

'No, I'm fine. Thank you.'

I went to my unit, unlocked the door and slid in. Took a few breaths. Dropped my shoulders. Wiped my damp armpits on some kitchen roll. The meter was ticking. I only had an hour for lunch. I needed to get going.

I picked up three of the boxes going to journalists and carried them out. I wanted to lock my door, but it would have been far too suspicious.

Alan was chatting to the driver, who'd turned the engine off and got out of the taxi.

'Let me,' said the driver, taking the pile out of my arms. He put them in the boot. I went to get the next batch. Alan, shamed into helping, stubbed out his cigarette and followed me inside.

'How many more have you got?' he asked.

I had no answer. My mind was desperately trying to think of a way to stop him stealing another glance at my bomb-maker's den. Pressure cookers, empty cold-pack wrappers, packing materials . . .

'I'm not sure . . .'

The phone rang in his pocket.

'Go ahead and get it,' I said. 'I can manage.'

'Suit yourself.' He carried on past my unit towards his office.

I took the other three out to the taxi and ran back to get the heavy one – the bomb – locking the door as I left.

I jumped in the back, super-relieved to be seeing the back of Alan.

'Where to?'

I gave the driver the address of the shop where SendEx would, as per my paperwork, be expecting to pick up the parcels. He parked on double yellows, right outside, with his hazard lights flashing.

Between us we carried the boxes into the drop-off shop and stacked them by the till.

'Thank you,' I said as he left with his fare and a small tip.

I handed over the parcels to the shop assistant, one

at a time. The guy was very slow. Checking everything. He was so intent on the task he didn't seem to notice me. Good. I studied him. Six foot, slopey-shouldered, a name tattooed on the inside of his wrist.

The fourth parcel, addressed to the chief exec of the drone manufacturer, was the loaded one. An X-ray would reveal exactly what it was, but there wasn't time to screen every single parcel. Fate was in charge of that aspect, but having Gadget Man down as its sender gave it its best chance.

'Next?'

He processed the last three and gave me the receipts.

It was surreal – as easy as returning an unwanted kettle to Tesco Direct. Yet in a day's time six journalists were going to be dropping everything to cover the story. Maybe one of them would make it their life's work to stop the drone wars – there was a constant stream of new material.

Eighteen male labourers, including a boy, were killed when missiles struck a tent they'd gathered in for their evening meal.

'Can I get you anything else?' asked the man on the till.

'No, thank you.'

I had twenty minutes before I was due back at work. Food was out of the question – I'd choke for sure. Instead, I went into Harvey Nicks and looked at all the cashmere jumpers, pretending to choose one for

Liam. It was frivolous but kept me occupied. The alternative was to dwell on what I'd just done, and that was out of the question. In between comparing shades of baby blue and turquoise, I tried to remember all the stuff Sayge had quoted about how nothing changes without a struggle. But already something like a conscience was bothering me. The bomb wouldn't explode on its own. If I didn't ring the number, it would just be a full-up pressure cooker . . .

And I'd have ruined my whole life for nothing, said the part of me I was more used to hearing. And kids and grandparents and mums and dads would carry on dying in the most despicable way . . .

I remembered Lamyah taking my hand that first day in Yemen, when the strangeness was overwhelming . . . Her hand was nothing more than fertiliser now.

56

I had to force myself to walk back into the building. Until I could see on the SendEx tracking system that the parcels had cleared American customs, I needed to keep Saffron Anderson doing what she did. But it wasn't easy. I was as pale as a ghost. And struggling to hold it all together. It was nothing like the exhilaration I'd felt when the drone was in my control.

I stared at my screen without seeing. Looked across at Elisa but couldn't find anything to say. A wave of nausea came over me.

I went to the loo and sat on the seat.

If I didn't get a grip, people would notice.

I washed my hands. In the mirror above the sink I could see my old self starting to come through. The blonde highlights had grown out and darkened, and my fringe had become so long I'd had to change it to a side parting and tuck it behind my ear. Memories hovered in my peripheral vision, but I didn't let them come into focus.

'Seeing Freddie tonight?' I asked Elisa as I sat back down at my desk. Steady voice.

'Yes, but not till you've finished with him.'

It took me a sec.

'Oh . . . I'm glad he's taking our house meals seriously.'

'It suits me too — I'm having my hair cut.'

I needed to get mine cut too. When Dronejacker was hurtled back onto the front page, the press would have a field day. This time I'd be the subject of an Interpol Red Notice — only used for the most deadly criminals. At that point, I needed to look as unlike Samiya and Saffron as possible. Red hair, blue contact lenses, maybe I'd get a tattoo on my neck and ear stretchers, and wear vintage leather and Dr Martens.

'I'll make sure tea's early,' I said.

The small talk helped the afternoon pass. Liam was in a meeting, which was a blessing. I didn't want him interrogating me about my strange mood. There was only tomorrow to get through, and then I'd never see him again. It was like being a suicide bomber, except, instead of heaven for the faithful, I had the prospect of a life where no one would ever truly know me.

Before I left the office, I input the tracking numbers from my receipts to see where the parcels were. Safely on their way to the freight terminal at the airport, as expected. I didn't feel pleased. I felt numb.

The meeting-room door was shut, but I glanced through the window as I passed by. Liam was standing up, shirtsleeves rolled to his elbow. He finished what he was saying and smiled at the audience. I looked away.

As I walked home I ran through the timetable.

If it all went according to plan, the journalists would receive their parcels between noon and five, local UK time, tomorrow. The bomb was scheduled to arrive before nine in the evening on Thursday. I'd added a command to the SendEx tracking system so that when the chief exec, or his wife, signed for the package a notification SMS would automatically be sent to my phone. All I had to do was make the call to the detonator and wait for the connection.

Bang!

As soon as I knew the bomb was on an American truck, I needed to get well away from Leeds. I tried to imagine myself on the train to Edinburgh, flushed with success. But couldn't get rid of a sense of doom. Was it leaving Liam? Or the memory of taping the last label on the heaviest of the boxes? Knowing what that meant.

Distract yourself, Saffron.

Food.

I cycled through recipes in my head.

In Sainsbury's I bought all the ingredients for Thai green chicken curry. Making the paste would take a while without a food mixer. Suited me.

Freddie came home to find me crushing coriander seeds in a mortar and pestle.

'You've got a good technique going there, Saff.'

'Plenty of practice,' I said.

He watched me peel, grate and chop.

'Sorry about Friday,' he said as I was zesting a lime.

'No need to apologise.'

The paste was starting to smell good, much better than any bought version.

'Elisa told me off,' he said.

'What for?'

It was very unlike Freddie to be so serious. Our relationship was based on banter.

'She said if you have secrets, it's no one else's business.'

'She's right,' I said.

'I should have known better. After all, I'm really a Russky spy.'

That was more like it.

Dinner was ready by a quarter to seven. Polly was much more talkative than normal because her boyfriend had agreed to move to Leeds.

'He's going to start looking right away,' she said.

'Don't forget to give me notice if you're moving out,' said Freddie.

It was *my* last night, but he didn't know it. I did a mental inventory of my room. No more than ten minutes and I'd be ready to go.

'Great curry, Saffron,' said Polly.

'Thanks.'

I managed to eat my whole bowl, partly because it didn't need much chewing or swallowing, and partly because sitting with the two of them gave me a false sense of normality. If I could keep hold of that, maybe I'd survive the next forty-eight hours. The most important forty-eight hours of my life.

57

Polly cleared up as per the agreement. Freddie went to change before his 'date' with Elisa. I went to my room. The proof of my next alias was where it had been ever since I came to Leeds, hidden under the rigid bottom of my rucksack. I put my cash there too. I wasn't taking much else. A few summer clothes to keep me going. My purse with the precious photo tucked out of sight. My all-important phone with the number of the other phone – the one taped to the pressure cooker – stored under B (for Bomb).

I ran through the shape of the next day, getting it straight in my head.

Act like it's a normal day at the office, check the status of the parcels periodically.

As soon as the parcels have cleared the airport, leave work saying there's a family crisis and you might be away for a few days. Knowing your situation, no one will dare question what that means.

Empty Saffron's bank account on the way home.

(Home – where would home be next?)

Pick up the rucksack and some clothes.

Leave a note for Freddie with the same excuse.

Get to Leeds train station tout de suite.

Quadcopters and warnings delivered to journalists Wednesday afternoon UK time.

Chaos.

Wait for text confirming parcel signed for Thursday evening UK time.

Call the number.

The last step didn't need itemising. I'd been building up to it for nearly two years. I knew what it was.

I heard the door slam shut and Freddie whistle his way into the distance. Ran a bath and dunked my whole body in it. I tried to enjoy the feeling of the hot water, but relaxing was out of the question. I gave up, put on my checked pyjama bottoms and a maroon vest and sat on my bed.

I had a whole evening to spend torturing myself by over-thinking the bomb, the fallout, my life, drone pilots, victims . . .

I went downstairs, hoping for some mind-numbing telly. Polly was playing music – couldn't tell what. I shut it out with the living-room door.

The controls were scattered among the furniture as usual. I turned on the set, the amp and the cable box.

The picture sprang to life. I pressed Guide and up came the TV schedule. I scanned the titles. The amp continued to play the soundtrack of whatever channel Freddie was last tuned to.

'So, Dan, how did you feel when the extradition order was withdrawn?'

I can't have heard right. Nerves getting the better of me. But I pressed Back just the same.

There was Dan Langley – tall, skinny, dark hair, dark T-shirt – sitting on a sofa, being interviewed by a woman with neat blonde hair and clever glasses. I sat cross-legged on the floor, bang in front of them.

'It felt incredible,' he said. 'I was sitting with my mum and then my lawyer turned up and said it was all over. I would've cried . . . but my girlfriend was there.'

I pressed the button for programme information, desperate to understand what I was watching.

It was a documentary called *Faces of Extradition*, following the cases of four Britons who were wanted in other countries. I didn't know whether to stay or run. My pulse was so fast it was more of a flutter than a beat.

Think, Saffron.

'Did you really believe you were about to be extradited to the United States and tried?' asked the interviewer.

'I did. It's been all over the news, so there's no point denying anything – I *was* guilty of hacking the drone.'

'To be clear, Dan, it was a military drone.'

He grimaced.

I decided I needed to watch. At least then I'd know what they were saying about me, if anything. No one knew anything about the bomb. It was coincidence that the programme was on tonight of all nights –

nothing more sinister. Weird, though. Dan on telly one day, Dronejacker all over it the next.

Dan gave a short explanation of how he met 'Angel', and his surprise when I turned out to be a girl.

'It's hard to explain how you can end up close to people you've never met in real life, but we did. Finding out Angel was a girl was like . . . what the hell?'

I'd only ever seen photos of him where he looked like a bit of a dork – but he was actually quite cute.

The interviewer was keen to know how he felt about Angel now.

'It's difficult,' he said. 'I know she tried to fire a missile at London and I should hate her, but if someone massacred my family, I don't know how I'd feel. I know I'm meant to condemn her but . . . we got on.'

Despite the fact that I was in shock at hearing myself discussed on telly, his comments trickled through to the memory of all the fun we'd had together. Of how much I'd liked him, until . . .

The interviewer turned to face me.

'Angel, whose real name is Samiya . . .'

I listened to her summarise my story, from growing up in Buckingham to the collateral murders to the foiled drone strike, which I was 'alleged' to have master-minded. I relaxed ever so slightly. 'Alleged' was good. No new information.

'Dan, it was your actions that led to the discovery of Angel's base in a house in Norfolk. Your bravery.'

Dan described, in a deadpan fashion, how he'd

located my mobile phone – but it still sounded stratospherically clever. She didn't comment, presumably because she didn't understand, instead moving on to the fact that I was still 'at large'.

Her final question to Dan was, 'Angel has disappeared – she's presumed to be in the Middle East. Do you think she might be out there planning another revenge attack?'

Stupid question. What did he know!

'I hope not. Can I just say that I only agreed to be interviewed to have a chance to say sorry to my family, to Ruby and to the people of London who were scared that day. I —'

The camera cut back to the interviewer.

'Thank you, Dan.'

She was getting ready to move on to the next extradition story, after the ad break.

I thought I might make a cup of tea, but then another face filled the screen and I had to smother the urge to scream.

58

'Hugo, you were a good friend of Samiya's.'

'That's right. We met when I joined her school in Year 11.'

He'd taken Dan's place on the sofa. Wearing an immaculate white shirt, sitting with one leg casually crossed over the other, he was clearly loving his moment in the spotlight.

Stupid me.

I'd seen the documentary about the White Widow. That was the sort of thing journalists did. Interview old school friends, neighbours . . . parents . . .

Please, not my parents.

Hugo described how, after the drone attack in Yemen, I went from being a popular girl to a loner.

'My sister and I used to talk about her a lot.' He turned to give the camera the benefit of his good looks. 'We were worried about her.'

Two minutes' worth of chatting with no substance and it seemed she was done with Hugo.

I held my breath, waiting to see who else they'd persuaded to talk about me . . .

Lucy? No she would never do that.

. . . but the interviewer started summing up the case.

'Dan Langley is yet another victim of the unequal Extradition Act. British courts were satisfied that Dan was duped by the real criminal, whom he knew as Angel, yet the Home Secretary allowed . . .'

The screen switched to show a photo of a gorgeous couple. A pale boy with blond hair and beautiful eyes, and a girl with shiny dark hair and eyes, coffee-coloured skin, and a smile on her lips.

It was the one Hugo'd taken of us in his bedroom, our heads on his pillow.

I tuned back into the words.

'After the break, *Faces of Extradition* will delve into the life of . . .'

I needed to react, but none of my synapses were firing.

My face was on the television.

It wasn't a blurred newspaper photograph, but a glossy close-up.

Someone would recognise me.

Move, Saffron.

I ran upstairs, tore off my pyjamas, pulled on a dress, grabbed my rucksack, shoved my phone and purse in the front pocket and zipped it up. Clothes I could do without.

The doorbell rang. I froze. Considered climbing out of the window.

Don't overreact.

It rang a second time.

'I'll get it!' shouted Polly.

I stood still. Praying for it to be a chugger.

'Saffron! It's for you.'

The most important thing was to stay calm. The photo had only just appeared on the telly – my visitor couldn't have seen it.

Breathe.

I walked downstairs to the kitchen, knowing it could only be one person. I should have expected him after our stilted chat earlier.

'He's fit,' whispered Polly as I passed her on the stairs.

I didn't respond. I needed to get rid of him – that was all I could think of.

'Hi,' said Liam, kissing me. 'I was out running and thought I'd pop in.'

My smile was as plastic as Barbie's.

'You don't mind?'

I shook my head.

'I know you said you were cooking, but I saw Freddie in the park, so I figured . . .'

Say something, Saffron.

'He's gone to meet Elisa.' I raised an eyebrow. 'Even put on a clean shirt!'

'Is that a pointed comment?' Liam looked down at his sweaty Nike vest.

'I could come round to yours later, if you like – when you're clean.'

'Or you could come with me now,' he said, his hand round the back of my neck, about to kiss me again.

I wriggled away. Everything was coming crashing down around me. Minutes counted.

'I was about to have a bath. I'll come in an hour.'

I sounded completely wooden – he could tell something was up.

I made myself lean across and kiss him.

'Go away and wash!'

That was better – more like me.

'All right. Whatever you say.'

He gave me an odd look, with his head tilted slightly over. *What's going on?* it said.

'Bye, then.'

He opened the door and was gone.

I raced back upstairs to get my bag. On the way back down Polly poked her head out.

'Everything all right?'

'Fine. That was my boyfriend, Liam. I'm going over to his.'

'He looked nice. How long have you been —?'

'I need to get going. I've . . .' My mind was blank. I pushed past her.

'OK. See you.'

I went out of the kitchen door and walked, with my head down, towards Woodhouse Lane to catch a bus. There was only one thought in my head – get away from Leeds.

'Saff!'

It was Mack. He was standing on the other side of the road, talking to Liam.

'You were on the telly!' he shouted.

Liam was in front of me in an instant, blocking my way, with Mack close behind him. I had nothing to say, so I waited for him to speak.

'Mack says you're —'

'The Dronejacker,' said Mack. 'You need to get away, Saff. You were on the telly. My mum rang the cops. You need to go.'

There was no time to try to persuade Liam that it was all a mistake. I'd already wasted ten – or more – minutes getting out of the house.

'Let me go,' I said. 'It's not what it seems, but until I can prove that I need —'

Looking at Liam's face was unbearable.

'I don't understand . . .'

A car turned onto Brudenell Road and accelerated past us. It was the police. As soon as they got to the house, Polly would say I'd just left and they'd be on my tail.

I pushed past Liam and ran.

59

I sprinted up Brudenell Road towards the park. Liam must have taken a moment to react, but was soon right behind me, his trainers thumping the pavement. I ran straight across Hyde Park Road without looking. A car swerved to avoid me – horn blaring. Liam had to wait to cross, giving me a badly needed few seconds' lead.

I ran across the grass. My chest was tight, my breathing heavy. If I could cut the corner and get to Woodhouse Lane, there was a chance I could dodge the traffic, lose them in the streets down by The Swan with Two Necks and make it to the taxi company that used a Portakabin as its HQ.

'Saffron, wait!' shouted Liam.

I willed my legs to go faster, but as the main road came into view I could see a police car, blue lights flashing. I changed direction, but there were more lights flickering through the trees.

I was trapped.

I couldn't think where the bomb was. Nine hours into its journey – did that mean it was in the sky? Or already landed?

It didn't matter. I couldn't let it all be for nothing. It was where it was.

As I turned round to face Liam, I shouted, 'Keep away!'

He stayed right where he was, maybe ten metres from me.

Mack – his little legs whirring like a cartoon – caught up.

'Saff!'

He looked like he was going to run over to me, but Liam grabbed his shoulder.

'Stay with me, mate.'

I slipped the rucksack off my back and held it in front of my chest, keeping my eyes on Liam's face, but not seeing him. If I'd had the phone in my hand, I could have called the number already, but it was in the zipped pocket – for safekeeping.

Before I had a chance to do anything else, a circle of police – five, no six – appeared from nowhere.

'Samiya, my name's Mike,' said a policeman in a blue shirt, walking slowly forward and stopping beside Liam. 'I need you to put the bag down and put your hands in the air.'

'Stay away!' I shouted, keeping the bag where it was. 'I'm not Samiya.'

'All right,' said Mike, before turning to Liam. 'I need you to move back, please, sir.'

'No,' said Liam. 'I'm staying here.'

Mack stayed glued to Liam's side.

'For your safety, if you and the boy could —'

'I said *no*.'

I took advantage of the moment, swung the ruck-sack so it was under my arm and unzipped the pocket.

Mike didn't like that one bit.

'Put the bag *down!*'

'Put it down, Saff!' shouted Mack, a cry in his voice.

The circle crept forward. I was aware of a hum in the background. The sound of passers-by stopping to watch, back-up teams, a journalist – alerted by Twitter . . .

The sound of a situation developing.

It had been fifteen minutes at most since my face had appeared on the telly. Too short a time for there to have been any verification. I was a suspect. No more. Nice policemen from Yorkshire wouldn't do anything rash.

'Please, Saffron,' said Liam.

'Saffron,' said Mike, 'do as I say and we can sort this out. Put the bag down.'

The voice was commanding. It made me want to obey. But I couldn't fail again. Who was I, if I gave up on the one thing that had defined me for so long?

A movement to the left caught my eye. A policeman moved to make space for a man wearing a white shirt and one of those black bulletproof vests. He raised his rifle – an MP5 Carbine – to shoulder height and pointed it at me, then adjusted it slightly. I didn't look behind, but sensed a second marksman had taken up position there.

I'd never considered that I might die. Surely no one would shoot a teenage girl . . .?

The fear was like something pressing on me. Heavy. Yet my thoughts were light, flighty, leaping about.

Death was sometimes the price . . .

One girl might have to sacrifice herself for the greater good. But not before she'd made her point . . .

My fingers were so close to the trigger, but so were theirs.

I needed to take control. But it was hard . . .

What would they do if I took out my phone? Everyone knows a phone can be a detonator.

I counted down in my head from five, building my courage.

Five . . .

Four . . .

Three . . .

Two . . .

I reached into the pocket and grabbed the phone, dropping the bag.

'Hands in the air!' screamed the man.

I did as he said, pressing the four digits of my pass-code with my thumb.

'Saffron! No!' I heard Liam shout.

There was a stillness. An unreal quiet. As though the air itself was holding its breath.

'Drop the phone *now* or we *will* shoot!' yelled Mike.

'Nooooo!' screamed Mack. As I looked up, he broke free from Liam's hold and ran towards me. It was the diversion I needed.

I pressed –

Phone

Contacts

B

The call connected instantly.

I locked eyes with Liam.

Heard the shot ————

Have you read the other side of the story?

Piccadilly
P R E S S

Thank you for choosing a Piccadilly Press book.

If you would like to know more about our authors, our books or if you'd just like to know what we're up to, you can find us online.

www.piccadillypress.co.uk

You can also find us on:

We hope to see you soon!